Poolside Promises

A sweet,
second chance romance

Kasey Kennedy

Other Books by Kasey Kennedy:

IN BLOOM SERIES:
Peonies for Paige
Dahlias for Dominica
Lilies for Lauren
Tulips for Tilly
Wildflowers for Anna Lee

MISTLETOE KISSES SERIES:
Mistletoe for Tricia

SEASIDE BAY SERIES:
Poolside Promises
Beachside Bliss (coming soon)

To Tracy Butler,
Our vacations together are some of my favorite memories!

Chapter 1

Sunscreen. Check. Magazines. Check and double check.

Linda Brees tossed the items into her large, yellow and white-striped tote bag. As soon as her friend, Sorcha, returned from the grocery store where she'd gone to restock their diet cola and snacks, they would go to the pool to relax in the Florida sunshine.

Linda's Uncle Paul owned the condo they were staying in. He'd offered it to Linda for any time, and she was taking advantage of his generosity by staying for three full weeks. It wasn't all fun and sun. She'd promised her boss, Grady, that she would monitor things for his real estate business while she was in Florida. They had a daily call around lunchtime, but it could shift based on Grady's needs and the Florida weather.

The Florida Gulf Coast was the perfect place to sort out a couple of big issues: number one, how was she ever going to get a date for her sister's wedding in two and a half months? And number two, what was she doing with her professional life?

Sure, what to do with one's life seemed like the bigger existential issue to wrestle with, but Linda was more worried about the looming deadline for finding a date to the wedding. It had the more urgent time pressure.

Her dating life was nonexistent, and a wedding date came with a lot of expectations. Her family would be there, and they would be looking at her to get hitched next.

They would be extra-attentive to Linda's date, and she didn't want to take any attention away from her sister. To fly under the radar, she hoped for a date that was attentive, good-looking, and under forty. Ideally, under thirty, but sometimes you have to take what the universe gives you.

As for her career, she loved her job, and she loved her boss, but she was feeling restless. It might be time for a change. She was feeling her "career clock" ticking.

After a couple of weeks alone in the sun, she might come up with solutions for both. A girl could dream.

Dream big and execute the plan. She tucked lip balm into the side pocket of her beach bag.

Walking into her bedroom, she put her laptop and notebook on top of the dresser. She changed into her white and pink-polka-dot bikini, threw her colorful paisley cover-up over her head, and slipped into flip-flops. She strolled towards the balcony door and stepped outside.

The sun was beginning its descent, but it was still high in the sky. At this time of day, the sunlight hit the water at such an angle that it reflected in her eyes. She slid the large black sunglasses from the top of her head to her nose. Inhaling deeply, she let the salty smell of sea-life fill her lungs. That's why she loved coming here. The wind, the water, and miles of sand.

Her parents, both educators, had brought the girls to this beach every June to celebrate the end of another successful school year.

Seaside Bay was a short drive south of Clearwater, nestled between several waterways and the gorgeous white sand beach to the west.

Linda was looking forward to the afternoon on the beach with Sorcha. They would swim and tan at the pool, then move to the beach when the building blocked the sun. Then they would come back to the condo to shower and get ready for an evening of fun, dinner, and a few tequila shots. Sorcha would only be here for two more days, so they would make the most of their last few evenings together.

The door to the condo opened and closed, and Linda left the bedroom to help Sorcha put groceries away.

"Hey, hey," Sorcha called as she put two large shopping bags on the counter. "I'm back!"

"Perfect timing," Linda said, peeking into the closest grocery bag. "I finished with my work and am ready to hit the pool."

"Thank the stars! Girl, I've been ready for hours." Sorcha began pulling fruit and snacks from the grocery bags. "I don't want to leave Sunday!"

"I wish you could stay longer." Once Sorcha left, Linda would be alone for the last two weeks of her "working vacation". She didn't mind being there alone—she had stayed in this condo in Seaside Bay many times over the years and was familiar with the cute coastal town—but she'd miss Sorcha's adventurous and outgoing personality.

"Ditto and then some! But I only get a week off. I don't get to make my own rules like some people I know." Sorcha shook her head, and her thick, blonde hair swished across her shoulders. She wore a pair of large, blue-leather teardrop earrings that she had made.

They were constantly looking for new side hustles. Sorcha's latest focus was on handmade jewelry, while Linda preferred to create printables. She designed and uploaded her templates, which people could buy and download. She didn't have to pack and ship anything like Sorcha.

Linda loved trying new things and earning extra cash. Her primary job as Grady's office assistant was great. It offered the flexibility to work remotely and came with health insurance.

"That's what you get for going into education," Linda replied. Having parents and a sister in education, Linda felt she knew the pros and cons of that career. "You knew the rules when you decided your degree."

"Uh, huh. Oh, hey!" Sorcha tossed a bunch of bananas into the large, blue-glass fruit bowl shaped like a fish that sat on top of the counter. Linda winced, thinking about the bruises they'd find on them tomorrow.

"What?"

"I rode up in the elevator with the hottest, and I mean hottest, guy I've seen this entire trip!"

Linda paused, holding the bag of Skittles she was about to put in her tote bag. "Was he delivering something? Everyone on this floor is my parents' age or older."

"No, he was pulling a couple of suitcases. Maybe he's staying with his grandparents. He was *not* old."

Linda's mind was whirling. She thought she knew everyone in this twenty-four-unit condominium building. When she stayed, she often volunteered to help Meridian, "Meri", the building manager, with different activities—shuffleboard games, bingo, trivia night, and dances. There was a large lounge on the first floor with space for the building's gatherings.

She'd even met the most recent residents, the Wilkersons, on Tuesday, when they'd asked for recommendations on where to eat (she'd suggested the Streamwood restaurant) and where to get little miscellaneous items between trips to the large grocery store, which was twenty-five minutes away (she told them about Franki's Sundries, two blocks away).

Who could Sorcha have seen in the elevator?

"Did he get off on this floor?" Linda asked.

"Yes! He went in right next door."

Oh, no. Oh, no. This is not good. It had to be Mason Hauser. When planning this trip, Linda had asked her Uncle Paul if any of the Hauser family would be in Florida at the same time. He said he'd checked with Mr. H., and no, they wouldn't be there.

Linda pushed the tote bag to the floor and plopped down on the wicker barstool, her heart racing. "What did he look like?"

Sorcha tilted her head and held her hand several inches over her head. "Tall. Maybe six-one. Broad shoulders. Muscular. Looked like he works out. He was tan, too. So, hot."

From what Linda had heard from Erin, Mason's sister, Mason's most recent nursing rotation had been in Southern California. That could explain the tan.

Linda groaned, putting her head down on her forearms. "No!"

"What?" Sorcha held out her hands and turned them palm side up. "Who is it?"

"It has to be Mason." Nervousness propelled Linda off the bar stool. She paced the length of the counter, tapping each of the four barstools as she passed.

"I don't know why you are sounding upset. Did I mention how hot he is?"

"You did. But..." She paused. How much did she want to share with Sorcha? She'd known Mason most of her life. They'd tried dating twice, but it hadn't worked out. She and Sorcha were on vacation; no sense in getting into the what-could-have-been and what-almost-was Mason stories. The only thing Linda worried about was Sorcha becoming interested in Mason. That would be too weird.

Simple. Keep it simple.

"Mason and I dated once upon a time. It didn't work out. Please don't fall for him. It would be too weird for me. Let's just try not to run into him again and go enjoy ourselves."

Sorcha was looking at her with a raised eyebrow. "I don't recall the name Mason ever coming up when we've talked about past boyfriends before."

"Really? Odd. Must have slipped my mind." Not true. Mason had never slipped her mind. He took up a lot more space there than she cared to admit. "Well." She stood. "Anything else to put away? I'm ready to soak up some rays."

Sorcha looked down. "No, that's it. I'll pack the cooler. But don't think you're getting away with changing the subject. You are going to have to share more details. I'm your roommate and bestie. I need to know everything about this Mason guy."

Sorcha opened the freezer door and grabbed all six trays of ice cubes. Linda grabbed the blue soft-sided cooler from the closet. She set it on the counter next to Sorcha. Sorcha launched into a story about the people she'd spoken to at the grocery store as she twisted the ice-cube trays into the cooler. She'd set the empty trays on the counter, and Linda would refill and put them back in the freezer.

Linda half-listened to Sorcha's story. She heard enough to make noises and laugh when appropriate, but she'd never be able to repeat anything that Sorcha had said later. She kept thinking about Mason being next door. How long would he stay? Would they run into each other? What would they say to each other if they did?

She'd avoided him for the last six years. Luckily, his decision to move frequently instead of staying close to home in central Illinois had helped. Plus, they were too old to vacation with their families or attend birthday parties anymore. When they'd seen each other last, it was a few days after their college graduation parties. The last hurrah.

Linda had thought that evening was going to turn out much differently than it had. They'd been dating for over a year. Linda told him she loved him and was certain he'd say it in return. Instead, he'd told her he'd accepted a nursing position in Atlanta and would leave in two days.

He'd broken her heart before; she wouldn't let it happen again.

Chapter 2

His two suitcases clip-clopped over the threshold. Mason was relieved he was finally 'home' in his family's vacation condo. His relief vanished when he realized how hot and stuffy it was inside. He was on a mission this trip to install a smart thermostat the family could control remotely. It would have been nice to turn on the air-conditioning before his flight left San Diego so he could have walked into a cool space.

He let go of the suitcase handles and strode the three paces to the offending ancient thermostat and turned on the air. He set the temp at a low, low sixty-three degrees. His eyes swept the room. He hadn't been here since Christmas, but nothing had changed.

The white-tiled floor gleamed as soon as he turned on the lights. His mother had painted every wall of this condo either a strong cerulean or a soft baby blue right before her cancer diagnosis.

The expected Florida decor filled the space. The last theme his mom had chosen was sea turtles. There was a large painting created by a local artist on the wall above the couch featuring a chaotic scene of hundreds of baby turtles rushing towards the water. Mason thought it was too busy, but he'd grown accustomed to it, and it hardly registered anymore.

The cream-colored couches in the living room called to him. He'd love to lie down with the balcony door open and listen to the sounds of the gulls and waves as they lulled him to sleep. Nothing brought him as much peace as the sound of the Florida coast. This modest condo in Seaside Bay had been his place of refuge since he was a kid.

But it was too hot to lie down now. He'd start with a cold shower instead.

Five minutes later, he was in the shower, relaxing as the cool water ran over him. He was grateful to be here. Even more grateful to be here alone. The last hospital rotation in San Diego had been a grind. He wasn't sure if it was that particular hospital or that particular city that had worn him out. He was thinking it was the lifestyle. Putting down temporary roots every twelve to sixteen weeks for the past five years had finally lost its luster. Five years, seventeen states, twenty-four cities, and three suitcases.

Well, two suitcases and a large backpack.

He'd learned early on to take only the essentials. When the first rotation took him from Atlanta to Norfolk, he'd loaded up his car and purchased a cartop carrier to haul boxes of CDs, DVDs, and books. After his third move, he'd decided life would be easier with a laptop, a Netflix subscription, and an e-reader.

Slowly, he let go of all the nonessentials. By deciding to look for gigs in larger cities, he let go of the car in his second year. No car insurance, no parking fees, no gas. Better for the environment and his bank account.

By keeping his costs low and taking long shifts, sometimes two shifts, in twenty-four hours, he'd paid off his student loans in year three. He'd kept up a quiet competition with his sister to get out of student debt the fastest. And knew he'd won, though she didn't even know they were playing.

He'd been jealous of Erin when she got accepted to medical school. She'd followed in their dad's footsteps by pursuing medicine. Mason had also planned to but seeing how the nurses cared for his mom as she'd battled cancer had inspired him to pursue nursing instead.

Yes, the doctors were important, too. They analyzed the facts, took input from mom and the nurses, and decided about care. But the nurses were the ones that held hands, encouraged, cheered, and did so many other things that made hospital visits and stays better. Watching them, he knew nursing was his true calling.

He knew his mom was proud of him, and that was all that mattered. His dad and sister's teasing never pierced the shell he'd pulled around himself.

Drying off, he thought about the woman he'd met in the elevator. She said she was staying with a friend, and he'd seen her go into the condo next door. That meant she was here with Laurel or Linda. He wondered which of the Brees twins was here.

Feeling refreshed, he dressed in a light gray T-shirt and a pair of dark gray gym shorts, and finally moved his suitcases from the foyer to the bedroom that faced the beach. He loved staying here when he could have this bedroom and sleep with the balcony door either cracked when the A/C was on or wide open when it was off. He loved being lulled to sleep by the sound of the ocean.

He unpacked and put fresh sheets on the bed, staring at it longingly. He was tired, but he knew if he crashed now, it would take him days to adjust to the time-change and the jet lag.

Fighting the urge to sleep, he grabbed his cell phone and called his dad.

In the kitchen, he filled a large glass with filtered water from the fridge. He glanced into the freezer and pulled out the ice trays, which held shriveled little slivers of ice. He tossed them in the sink as his dad answered.

"Hey, Mace." His dad sounded rushed. Oh, right, he would still be at work.

"Hey, Pops. I made it to the condo. Everything looks good." His dad always worried about break-ins or damage from nature when they were away for an extended time. As far as Mason knew, no one had been to the condo since New Year's when his dad and stepmom, Terry, had stayed.

"Good to hear. How was the flight?"

"Fine. No issues. Just an early start." Mason took a long drink of water, steeling himself for the next question. "Hey, I met a young woman in the elevator. She said she's staying next door with a friend. Next door being the Brees's place. Do you know if Laurel or Linda are down here?"

"Oh. Now that you mention it, a few weeks ago, Paul asked if any of us were going to be there. He said Linda was planning to go. That was before you decided to take a work break and stay, so I told him none of us would be there. So, yes. It must be Lindy."

Mason smiled, hearing his dad revert to the childhood nickname for Linda. It had been years since he'd heard it.

"Cool. That's cool. Hey, do you mind if I replace the thermostat while I'm here? We need to get with the times and get a smart one."

"How smart can a thermostat be?"

"OK, Boomer."

His dad chuckled. "You know I'm not a boomer. I'm Gen X. The forgotten generation."

"Whatever."

"I got to run, son. Enjoy your time off. Did you decide where you're going next?"

"Not yet. Hope to work that out soon. But I'm not thinking about anything for the next three days. I need to decompress."

They said goodbye, and Mason put the phone on the counter. He took his glass of water and went to the balcony. Outside, he leaned against the railing and surveyed the beach. Then he took a glance at the balcony to his right. No one was there, but there was plenty of evidence that someone was staying in the condo. The heavy outdoor chairs had large yellow cushions on them. Mason knew that when no one was there, the cushions were kept inside, out of the elements. He saw a coffee cup on the small table. That in itself told him Linda was there. Last he knew, Laurel could not stand coffee. Coffee had been one of his and Linda's things. They'd enjoyed making coffee runs several days a week when they were in college.

So, Linda was staying next door. And she'd asked if any of his family was going to be in Florida at the same time. He was sure she played it off as 'just curious' but Mason wondered if she still hoped to avoid him.

He couldn't blame her. He'd been an absolute jerk to her the last time he'd seen her. She'd declared she loved him, and he responded with "I'm leaving". He was sure she hated him even with six years behind them.

He told himself he'd been immature. At twenty-two years old, after having lost his mom the year before, he couldn't think straight half the time, let alone think about a long-term relationship.

He'd run from any sort of commitment. He couldn't commit to a city, a job, or a girl.

A seagull landed on the balcony's railing to his left and he turned his head to it. It seemed to look at him and nod. Mason nodded back. This is what he'd been needing. Time, the wind, the beach, and nodding to a seagull.

What he didn't need was Linda. Seeing her again would remind him of the worst mistake he'd ever made in his life—leaving her.

He'd thought that leaving would heal his heart. He'd hoped a change of scenery would help him forget the pain of losing his mom. Instead, moving frequently exacerbated his loneliness. Meeting new people, getting lost in new cities, and adjusting to new workplaces kept his mind busy, but the pain continued to follow. He hadn't left it behind.

But now Linda was *here*. Maybe it was fate. Maybe it was time to make amends and get reacquainted.

How many times had he thought about reaching out to her? A hundred? A thousand? It'd been six years. He thought about her constantly. What was she doing? Who was she seeing? Was she happy? Would she forgive him?

Maybe he'd find some answers in the next few days, while they were both in Seaside Bay. Perhaps he could leave the Sunshine State with a deeper tan, a sunnier disposition, and a restored friendship.

Chapter 3

Linda put her feet up on the lowest bar of the railing and scooted lower in her chair. Sorcha was still asleep, and by Linda's reasoning, would be for a couple of hours. They had partied it up the night before, but while Linda had switched to nonalcoholic beverages once they got to Crabbie's, one of their favorite local dive bars two blocks from the beach, Sorcha had carried on and was drunk with a capital "D" by the time they got home.

A loud squawk caught Linda's attention, and she looked up, watching the lift and dive of two large birds who appeared to be hunting for their breakfast.

Ruckus over, Linda turned back to the paperback novel in her hand. Her favorite thing to do in the morning was to read on the balcony while she watched the early morning shell seekers on the beach.

She loved to stroll to the beach and walk for miles, kicking the sand and looking for unique shells. It made her feel like a kid again. Carefree, safe, curious, and on an adventure. All those wonderful things that are lost with growing up.

As a kid, she and her twin sister, Laurel, would compete to see who could find the prettiest shells. Her whole life was a competition with her twin. Laurel had been born three minutes earlier than Linda and never let her forget who was older.

Or more driven.

Or more outgoing.

It was challenging playing second fiddle to her identical twin. At least there was no question who was prettier. That was a clear tie.

Laurel had even followed in the footsteps of their parents and become an educator, which sometimes made Linda feel like an outsider in her own family.

That was okay. Linda took her outsider role seriously. She loved forging her own path, standing out in her own way. Whether that was working in a company of two people versus an organization with hundreds or wearing unusual and vintage clothes, she was happy being her own person.

She turned the page and heard the unmistakable sound of a balcony door sliding open. She turned, thinking maybe Sorcha had fallen out of bed and was making her way outside. Instead, movement on the balcony next door caught her attention.

A moment later, two large coffee mugs advanced onto the balcony, followed by the muscular arms of the man next door. Mason.

There was no time to make an escape inside. *Shoot! I'm stuck!*

Looking at the two mugs in his hands, she wondered if he had a visitor. If another woman walked out onto the balcony behind Mason, Linda would book a flight home with Sorcha on Sunday and forgo the two additional weeks of planned "vacation".

Unable to look away, Linda blushed when Mason's eyes met hers. He smiled, that twisted half smile of his that always took her breath away. Strange that he still had that effect on her after all this time.

"Good morning, Lindy!" he called.

She groaned inwardly. She hoped Sorcha wouldn't hear the nickname and pick it up. "Morning."

"I brought you a cappuccino." Linda was stunned as he advanced towards her. There was a two-foot gap between their balconies. Mason had been brave enough to climb across it once when they were sixteen, but decided as he grew older that it was a silly stunt, four floors above the concrete sidewalk below. Too far to climb safely but not too far to hand something over.

"Really?" She stood and advanced towards him. She could take his coffee. She could pretend that the last time they'd seen each other he hadn't broken her heart.

"Yes. I talked Dad into getting one of those fancy coffee stations. It's a work of art. I need to get a few more supplies at the grocery store and I can make whatever fancy drink you desire. For today, I started with a regular cappuccino with a light foam, dusted with cinnamon sugar."

"Sounds divine. Thank you." She took the offered mug and leaned against the wall as she took a sip. "Yum. Delicious."

"Thank you!" He lifted his mug in a "cheers"-type salute and took a drink.

Linda studied him as he turned towards the water. He was more muscular than he'd been in college. He must have put on twenty pounds, all muscle. Sorcha wasn't kidding when she said he had a muscular physique. *She was right, he is hot. No wonder Sorcha went on and on about him.*

His hair was shorter. He'd begun wearing it past his shoulders in college, but now it was trimmed. The front was longer, and she imagined he probably kept it slicked back with a little gel. This morning, it was loose and being tossed with the breeze. She imagined running her hand through his hair and shook her head. It was not smart to let her mind wander there.

Keep it together! You will not fall for him again. You're not! Third time is never the charm, no matter what they say. I'm not. Falling. For him. Ever again! Wait, is that a Taylor Swift song? Sip your coffee. Act normal. Whatever that is.

Thirty seconds ticked by, and neither of them spoke. Linda studied his profile, searching for other changes in attitude or appearance. He seemed calmer. No longer a boy, but a man, comfortable and confident. She noticed a few fine lines around his eyes. A man who smiled a lot. She imagined he used that wonderful smile to cheer up his patients.

She'd known he'd be an excellent nurse. He was caring and charming. While his dad and sister were in an uproar when he'd pursued nursing instead of pre-med, Linda felt nursing fit him better and was proud when he'd bucked his dad's expectations.

She remembered countless nights studying with him, discussing their futures, their careers, their dreams and fears. They'd been such great friends, and when they tried the relationship thing for the second time in college, she'd felt it was the right time.

At twenty-two, she'd thought they were mature enough to finally commit to one another. They'd tried dating when they were sixteen, but quickly found they were too young and immature. Besides, they were always around their families, and the teasing from both sides ended up pushing them apart.

They'd entered college as friends, close friends, and Linda had been content with that. But when Mason's mom got sick, he needed Linda in a new way. She'd been there when he needed a shoulder to cry on when his mom took a turn for the worse. Several times.

"Well—" He finally broke the silence and turned towards her. "I hope we have time to catch up. How long are you staying for?"

"Two more weeks." *Shoot! Now that I've said it, I can't leave early.* At least a woman hadn't followed him out. He'd obviously made the coffee for her. "Did you see me out here?" *Dumb question. He must have. He'd brought out two mugs.*

"Yes." He nodded. "I met your friend yesterday and figured out you were here. This morning when I got up, I peeked out and saw you sitting here. Is your friend up?"

Linda sat back down and took another sip of the hot drink. "No, she won't be for a while."

"Late night?" Mason sat in the seat closest to her balcony so they wouldn't have to shout.

"Yes. Most of them are when Sorcha's around. My liver will appreciate it when she heads home on Sunday."

This was normal conversation. They could be friendly. Maybe he didn't remember the last time they'd spoken like she did. Maybe it was a bad memory he'd left in Illinois when he'd made his escape.

Mason turned towards her and laughed. "Yikes. I bet you two have been breaking hearts all around Seaside Bay."

Linda smiled but didn't answer. She didn't owe him any answers about dating. She ran through and quickly dismissed several topics—his family's health and news. She heard about that from her mom. The weather, too mundane; her career, too boring.

Mason didn't wait for her. "Wow. I can't believe we're here at the same time. It's been almost six years. Can you believe how fast it's gone by?"

"Six years in May," she responded.

"Right. Feels like yesterday."

"Really? I don't think so. It feels like a lifetime ago to me."

He nodded and took a sip from his mug. If it felt like yesterday to him, maybe he did remember the last time they were together. When she had embarrassed herself thoroughly, thinking they were ready to commit. She closed her eyes and leaned her head back against the chair cushion. She really wished she was leaving on Sunday.

Mason was feeling unmoored. He thought the ten hours of sleep he'd gotten would have given him a clear head and the ability to talk to Linda without it getting weird. He'd been very wrong.

She was acting civil enough, but he could tell the walls were there. Her smile didn't reach her eyes, and she spoke more softly than he remembered. Had it been a mistake approaching her this morning? Maybe he should have waited for her to approach him, if she wanted to.

But he couldn't. He'd been yearning to mend their friendship for years. And, if he was honest with himself, he'd dreamed of renewing their romantic relationship over the years, too.

He didn't think she was seeing anyone; he would have heard about it from his sister Erin if she was. Erin and Linda's sister, Laurel, were best friends and talked constantly. Erin usually told him when anyone in the Brees family had a cold, and he'd heard frequently about Laurel's wedding plans. She was getting married in June. He was told his invitation had arrived at his dad's home last month.

He wondered how Linda was feeling about Laurel's wedding. He hoped he'd have time to talk to her about it.

He cleared his throat. "What do you ladies have planned for today?"

"Well, it's Sorcha's last day and night here. If she's feeling like it when she gets up, we plan to drive to Clearwater for the day. See a different beach. She has an early flight and wants to pack before we go to dinner and go out."

"If she's flying in the morning," he said, "I recommend taking it easy on the drinking tonight."

"Yes, Nurse Mason," Linda answered dryly.

"Yeah, I deserve that. It's hard to step away from the job."

"Do you still like it?" Her voice was soft and hesitant.

"Love it."

"That's good." She looked down at the coffee cup in her hand.

He looked out at the water, and his eyes followed a boat on the horizon, traveling south. He wondered if they were sightseeing, or fishing, or doing something else.

It was good that he loved his job. It wasn't good that the constant uprooting and moving on were getting old. He thought more and more that it was time to unpack for good. Maybe buy a TV or get a pet.

"It is and it isn't," he finally responded. "I still love nursing, but I think it might be time to find a permanent position. Living out of a couple of suitcases no longer holds the appeal that it once did."

"I guess you've traveled a lot."

"I'll have to show you the printout that I carry. I've highlighted every city and state that I've lived in. It's an impressive map."

"I bet it is." Her voice was sad, and he had to strain to hear her over the sound of the surf.

Her head turned away from him. He appreciated the opportunity to gaze at her without her pretty, light blue eyes studying him. She was in a pale pink T-shirt and pink plaid pajama pants. They were a nice compliment to her bright pink hair that was pulled up in a messy bun.

She still took his breath away. Blond hair, purple hair, green hair, or pink hair, it wouldn't matter to him. She had been his first crush at twelve, and though the feelings had escalated and deescalated like a roller coaster over the years, a smile from her would still send his heart rate into overdrive. He hoped to see a genuine smile from her, preferably one he'd caused, soon.

Seeing her with bright pink hair didn't surprise him. She'd been experimenting with hair and makeup and clothes since she was fifteen. He always wondered if it derived from being an identical twin.

He admired her bold, creative personality. Erin told him that Linda's vivid hair color was driving Laurel crazy. She hated that they'd become the "wild twin" and the "conservative twin".

Linda always strove to be her own person and set herself apart from Laurel. He and Linda had spent hours over many nights complaining about their older sisters. His by two years, Linda's by a few minutes. Normal sibling rivalry stuff.

Ever since he'd learned that Linda was here, he'd played potential scenarios in his head. How would he approach her? Would he need to apologize right away? Should he act like the last six years were weeks, not years? So many potential outcomes, and no way to know how Linda would react to seeing him.

So far, things seemed all right. She hadn't left immediately, and she was drinking his coffee. Good signs. But she seemed reserved, distant.

He was sure it was because of how he'd left things six years ago, and he never had figured out a way to approach her again. He didn't deserve her friendship again yet, but he hoped he could show her he'd changed, matured. Perhaps they could find a way forward that wouldn't be awkward.

"Sounds like Sorcha's moving around," she said, turning back to him. She drank from the cup again, tilting her head back. He watched her swallow and admired her long neck. "I'd better get in there and see if she needs some aspirin."

She reached across the gap between their balconies to hand him the mug.

"Tylenol," he said.

She smirked. "Yes, Nurse Mason."

"Enjoy your day," he said. "Maybe we can go to dinner after your friend leaves, then we could catch up."

A cloud seemed to roll across her face. He could tell the suggestion made her uncomfortable.

"Yeah, sure," she said, but the shrug of her shoulders told him she wasn't excited about the prospect.

Chapter 4

Sorcha handed Linda the solid sunscreen stick used to put sunscreen on the scalp where their hair parted. Linda loved her large, floppy straw hat, but Sorcha insisted she needed the extra sunscreen on her head, even with the hat. Sorcha was fair-skinned, so she bathed in sunscreen to protect herself.

"All right. Now it's time to spill the tea," Sorcha said, adjusting herself on the beach blanket.

They were set up for tanning on the beach. Linda had brought a small speaker, an extra-large beach blanket that repelled sand, and a cooler. Sorcha had brought five bottles of sunscreen, thirteen magazines, and cooling towels. They had a reservation at two o'clock to go parasailing.

"What tea is that?" Linda asked, even though she knew this was going to be about Mason. Sorcha would never let a good story slide by her, and Linda had been tight-lipped the day before.

"The Mason tea. You know, like in a Mason jar." Sorcha roared at her own joke and the couple lying ten feet in front of them turned around. Sorcha waved at them and then turned back to Linda.

"Right. We're old family friends. My dad, his dad, and my Uncle Paul were all fraternity brothers in college. Uncle Paul, and Christopher, Mason's dad, bought the condos at the same time." Linda opened her book and pretended to read.

Sorcha paused a few moments before shaking her head. "No. No," she drawled. "I don't feel that's it. You're putting off a 'please don't ask about him because I'm secretly in love with him, and I want to tear off his clothes every time I see him' vibe."

"Now you're being ridiculous."

"Am I?" Sorcha pulled a margarita out of the cooler—margaritas they had made and packaged in reusable plastic pouches. The one she pulled out had "#MargLife" printed in a purple cursive font. She struggled to get a straw into the top.

"You are," Linda insisted. She adjusted her hat and put her sunglasses back on. "Hand me one of those."

"You're making this harder than it needs to be. Can't believe we're going to play twenty questions. But fine. Number one. You said you two dated once upon a time. How serious was it?"

"We dated twice upon a couple times and the first time, not serious at all. The second time was more serious. We dated our junior and senior years of college, but we broke up right after graduation."

Sorcha finally got the straw in the pouch, but a stream of liquid shot out and landed on her chest. She shrieked from the cold, and the couple turned again. "Do you want to join us back here?" she yelled at the couple. They turned back around. Sorcha dabbed at the liquid with her T-shirt. She then grabbed another pouch for Linda and handed it to her. "Ok. I need more details. Explain."

Linda took the offered beverage. "Well, we dated for a minute when we were in high school. We were sixteen, and we'd both started driving. I think dating was an excuse to drive more."

"That's lame."

"Yes," Linda laughed. "Tell me about it."

"I don't think that's all to this story. Go on."

"Well, that didn't last long. We lived about an hour apart and went to different high schools. We quickly became wrapped up in our own worlds again. Then we went to ISU together. We were close friends, study buddies for the first couple of years. But then his mom got sick, and things changed between us. We grew closer. I felt like he needed me, and I loved being the rock he relied on, you know?"

Linda paused and took a long drink of the margarita. Perfect. The fresh and sour taste flooded her taste buds. *Hey, watch it there. It's not even noon yet.*

"Yeah, yeah." Sorcha waved her hand in the air. "That sounds nice. What else? I bet he was fun in the sack. He's very muscular-ly."

Linda choked on the drink and her eyes watered. *Of course, she'd jump there.* "No, back then he wasn't built like he is now. And I wouldn't know about the other. It never happened between us."

Sorcha made a show of sighing and dropping her shoulders. "You are so boring. Did you kiss him at least? How was that?"

There were two options here. Stall, which would turn into a big deal in Sorcha's eyes, or give a brief answer and hope she would change the subject. "Yes, I've kissed him. No big deal."

"He's a good kisser?"

"Average. Guess we didn't have a lot of passion."

That wasn't true, but how could she explain it? Mason had been everything Linda had ever wanted and more. He'd been her closest confidant for nearly fifteen years. And then he was gone. That was a wound that might never heal. There was no sense in thinking about the way her mouth fit his perfectly. Memories of those kisses took her breath away.

"A guy like that screams passion to me." Sorcha finished her margarita and grabbed a bottle of water from the cooler. "So, I can't jump his bones?" Sorcha gave her a pouty smile with a mischievous look in her eyes.

"Absolutely not." Linda laughed at her roommate's antics, knowing she was teasing.

"Fine. I feel that you're holding something back. But I'll wait until you get liquored up, then I'll get you to spill."

Sorcha pulled a magazine out of her tote bag, and Linda relaxed. She opened her book and tried to read. But the image of Mason on the balcony this morning kept replacing the words on the page.

Their parasailing excursion would involve a boat ride. They had taken their tote bags and cooler to the car and only carried a single waterproof bag between them. They walked to the wharf where the boat was docked and met the newlywed couple who would be on the trip with them.

Once the crew members signaled it was time to go, Linda followed Sorcha onboard. She was thankful she'd pulled on the acupressure wristband that combated motion sickness before they took off. She was also thankful they'd each only had one margarita before getting on the boat.

Twenty minutes into the ride, the newly married man eagerly got into the harness and was released behind the boat. He whooped and hollered all the way up. His wife started out excited, but soon she was retching over the side of the boat. Linda had to turn away and kept her eyes on the captain of the boat while Sorcha helped the bride hold her hair back as she got sick.

Once they brought the man in, Linda was ready to go next. She figured it was now or never, and better to get off the boat, even if they would hike her two hundred feet into the sky, rather than stay on and listen to someone upchuck overboard.

She said a brief prayer as they pushed her off the back of the boat and picked up speed.

"You're never had a rope break, right?" she called as the boat accelerated and she floated into the air.

"Hardly ever!" the kid in a yellow T-shirt yelled.

Not comforting. She took a deep breath and tried not to think about the worst things that could happen.

"Serenity now!" she shouted, knowing no one could hear her. Reaching "cruising altitude", she couldn't hear the motor. It was uncannily quiet. High in the air, she looked around. There were several other ships this far from shore, and she counted those she could see. She quickly tired of that and put her heels together to form a "V", laughing to see that at this distance the boat fit between her feet. She held up the phone tethered to her wrist and clicked a couple of pictures. Then she surveyed everything around her, the blue water and blue sky. Here she was, flying like a bird. It was exhilarating! From now on, she would parasail every chance she got.

Far too soon, she realized they were pulling her down, and the boat steadily grew bigger the closer she got.

Sorcha was watching her come in and taking pictures. She jumped up and down as Linda's feet hit the small platform at the back of the boat.

"Linda, you looked amazing up there!" Sorcha said, rushing forward to give a high five.

"Thanks. It was amazing being up there. You are going to flip your lid!"

"Can't wait." Sorcha shimmied and winked at the guy in the yellow shirt as he held the harness out to her. "Take lots of pictures."

"I will!" Linda promised. "Enjoy!"

They buckled Sorcha in, gave her quick instructions, and tossed her off the boat. The young bride got sick again, which distracted the driver, and Sorcha's feet dipped into the water.

Oh, thank goodness that didn't happen to me! Linda quickly snapped a picture, even as she fretted at Sorcha's safety. Sorcha's eyes were double their normal size and Linda laughed as her friend was hoisted into the air as the boat hit another gear.

As they were hooking Sorcha up, the kid told her to look for large sea turtles in the water. He said that the colors of the parachute attracted them.

Linda groaned. *Why didn't he tell me that? I would have loved to see turtles.*

Thinking of turtles made her think about Mason and his family's condo. She'd been with his mom when she bought the turtle painting that hung in their living room. They'd been at a local farmer's market and met the artist selling her work. It had just been the two of them shopping, and Crystal had asked Linda which painting she should get. Linda had loved the colors in the turtle painting and had told Crystal so. When Crystal had bought it, it made Linda feel special to be listened to like that. She'd told Mr. Hauser if he ever thought about getting rid of the painting, she wanted to buy it from him. So far, he was unwilling to let it go.

Chapter 5

Hours later, Sorcha zipped her suitcase closed and declared herself packed. They'd returned from the beach, showered, and dressed for dinner. In a few minutes, they would walk to the fanciest restaurant in Seaside Bay, The Streamwood, for their last dinner together in Florida. After dinner, they would go to Crabbie's to drink, dance, and socialize.

Sorcha wore a low-cut white tank top and skimpy black leather shorts. She had on high-heeled sandals with thin black straps across her toes and around her ankle. Linda eyed them warily. She hoped she wouldn't be carrying Sorcha home from the bar later.

Linda wore a comfortable, loose-fitting maxi dress with spaghetti straps and a large fern pattern. It wasn't something she'd ever wear at home, but here in Florida, it felt fitting. Plus, she'd picked it up for only five dollars at a thrift store earlier in the week—score!

Applying pink lipstick, Linda checked her hair in the mirror. Sorcha had braided a fancy Dutch braid in Linda's hair and had woven in several strands of "fairy hair", which were essentially strands of green and silver tinsel. The colors complimented Linda's pink hair nicely. She felt like a rock star, if she was being honest.

"Have you seen my silver hoop earrings?" Sorcha asked, bursting into the bathroom.

"Not since this morning. You pulled them out when you parasailed. Are they in your tote bag?"

"Good call." Sorcha darted out.

Linda grabbed her glass of Moscato and left the bathroom. She walked her wineglass to the kitchen sink and glanced around for her purse. Hearing a door shut in the hallway, she wondered if it was Mason. She hoped they wouldn't run into him tonight. She worried Sorcha would grill Mason for information, information Linda wasn't ready to hear. Like, did he have a girlfriend? Where was he moving next? Why, in Mason's opinion, hadn't things worked out between him and Linda? Sorcha loved to meet new people, and she wasn't afraid of asking hard questions.

The short walk to the restaurant led them down the modest main street of Seaside Bay. They passed the pool and the parking lot of The Mockingbird, waited for two cars to pass through the intersection of Beachside Boulevard, gazed in the windows of Sunshine Sally's clothing boutique, passed the Sailfish Inn Bed and Breakfast, and popped into Bayside Books, where Linda purchased three new-to-her, used cozy mysteries.

An early afternoon storm cooled the air, and Linda regretted not bringing a sweater or light jacket.

As they exited the bookstore, Sorcha asked if she should get Linda's cats from Laurel's place when she returned home.

"No, let them stay with Laurel until I get back. I need to be indebted to her just a little bit more," Linda said, the sarcasm dripping from her tongue.

"You need to put your sister in her place." Sorcha threw her arm across Linda's shoulders. "I still can't believe she wants you to dye your hair for her wedding. No one will recognize you if you don't have pink hair!"

"Don't remind me. But she's the bridezilla to end all bridezillas so, lucky me." She shrugged. She understood her sister wanted her wedding pictures to remain framed on the walls of her home forever, and Linda wasn't sure she'd be happy seeing herself with pink hair at her twin sister's wedding twenty years from now either, but it was the principle of the thing. Why did her sister feel it was her right to demand that Linda color her hair?

Linda promised herself she wouldn't get jealous of Laurel. She loved her sister, but twenty-eight years of playing second fiddle to her twin was grating on her nerves.

She sighed as they entered the restaurant. At fifty-years-old, the Streamwood was the oldest operating business in the area. Linda loved its dark wood paneling, the old Hollywood style booths, and the smell of seafood and steak.

They sat near the western wall, which was a row of glass panels that could open to let in the gulf breeze, and tonight they were wide open. Seated, the young women ordered a calamari appetizer and two strawberry daiquiris. Once the server brought their drinks, they toasted to their last night in Florida together and promised each other it would be a fun one.

Feeling woozy after dinner and two daiquiris, Linda and Sorcha wobbled half a block closer to the condo building and entered the local dive bar, Crabbie's.

There was live music playing tonight, and the bar was hopping. Seemed like everyone under thirty-five years old within a twenty-mile radius was jammed into the space.

Sorcha led the way to the bar and found their favorite tender, Quincy, serving drinks. Quincy looked like he was old enough to be everyone's grandfather, but he claimed he was only forty-two. He was a transplant from the upper East Coast. He wouldn't say where exactly, but everyone suspected New Jersey, based on his dialect. Quincy was bald and seemed to be minutes away from a serious burn on his scalp. His piercing blue eyes held either laughter or a warning. There was no in-between. The tattoos covering his neck gave the final warning. Look, but don't touch.

Sorcha had been drooling over Quincy all week.

"What's up, ladies?" he asked, tossing the silly coasters with "Crabbie's - you can itch, but you better let us scratch!" logo at them and giving a sexy wink.

"Hi, Q. Two mojitos, and make them strong!" Sorcha called.

He nodded and stepped away.

"Don't forget you're flying home tomorrow morning. Early," Linda reminded her.

"Right. Right. This is my last drink with alcohol. That's why I asked for it to be strong." Sorcha scanned the room as her hips started swaying to the beat. The band was covering nineties hits tonight, and Linda knew they'd be on the dance floor soon.

Quincy brought the drinks, and Linda handed him a twenty. "My treat," she said to Sorcha. "To your last night in Florida!"

Sorcha clicked her glass, and they turned to look for seats. Every spot surrounding the bar was occupied.

Linda pointed to a tall table near the dance floor, and they made their way over. Perching on the seats, they looked around. Linda recognized many of the people. They'd been in the bar five nights that week. It was better than hanging out on the patio at the condo with the mostly retired residents. They were a lot of fun and great to talk to, but Linda and Sorcha preferred to let their hair down with people closer to their own age.

Before they had even finished their drinks, a man wearing a gold chain—instant turnoff for Sorcha—bought them another round. He became less of a turnoff for Sorcha, and she let him lead her to the dance floor.

Linda worried about the amount of alcohol her friend was drinking and asked the server for two glasses of water. She hoped dancing would burn off some of the alcohol.

Two hours, three drinks, and fifteen songs later, Linda decided it was time to leave. She checked the time on her phone and motioned for Sorcha to come off the dance floor. She did when the song finished.

"We should get going," Linda said, showing Sorcha the time display. "Have to get you to the airport in seven hours."

Luckily, Uncle Paul kept a car for anyone to use while staying in the condo. Linda didn't mind getting up and driving her friend to the airport, but if she didn't get some sleep soon, she'd consider calling a rideshare for Sorcha in the morning.

"But the band says they're playing until midnight!" Sorcha whined.

"That doesn't mean we have to stay."

"Aw, come on. We said we were going to get crazy tonight."

Linda shook her head. "No, we didn't."

"I think we should! I don't want to go home!" She stomped her heel to emphasize her point.

A man neither of them recognized approached. Linda gave him the side-eye. If he asked Sorcha to dance, she might not get her friend to leave.

"How are you beautiful ladies doing this evening? Can I buy you a drink?"

"Fine," Sorcha slurred. The man turned towards the bar.

"She means we're fine," Linda said. "Not fine for a drink. We need to leave."

He touched Sorcha on the forearm, and Linda wanted to swat his hand away. *How rude!* "The night is still young. Let's have some fun."

Sorcha gave a little whoop and pranced back onto the dance floor. Linda plopped into her seat and decided to give Sorcha five more minutes, then she was dragging her out the door, by Sorcha's silky blonde hair if she had to.

The smarmy man did not follow Sorcha to the floor. He put his hands on either side of Linda's chair and leaned over. The smell of alcohol on his breath instantly churned the contents of Linda's stomach.

"Hey, pretty lady," he slurred. "How about a dance?"

Linda shook her head slowly, making sure it was clear to him. "No, thank you. We have to get home. One of us has an early flight tomorrow."

"I'll take you home." He leaned even closer, and his hot breath flamed across Linda's cheek.

Another voice broke in, controlled and firm. "No. You won't!"

Mr. Smarmy suddenly jerked backwards. "What the..."

Linda looked behind him and saw Mason with his hand around the drunk guy's upper arm. She jumped out of her chair. "Don't!"

Mason looked at her and shook his head. "I won't hit him. Are you all right?"

The scuffle attracted the stares of everyone around them. Sorcha rushed over and put her arm around Linda. "What happened?"

"Let go!" Smarmy yelled at Mason.

Mason dropped his grip on Smarmy and looked at Linda. "Ready to go? I'd be happy to walk back with you ladies."

Linda swallowed and nodded. "That sounds like a good idea. Ready, Sor?"

Smarmy stalked off.

They made their way to the front door, and Quincy caught up to them. "You girls okay?"

"Yes," Linda answered. "We're good."

Addressing Mason, Quincy said, "Want a job as a bouncer? You've got the build and the eye for it."

"I'm not sticking around long enough, but thank you."

Outside, Linda realized adrenaline was still rushing through her veins. "Mason, where did you come from? I didn't see you in there."

"I was sitting on the far side of the bar."

"You were watching us?" Sorcha asked, swaying into Linda.

"Not intentionally. I noticed you a few minutes ago. I'd only been in there for a little bit. It was too nice to stay in the condo."

Sorcha nudged Linda with her shoulder. "Yes, you shouldn't stay cooped up. I'm leaving tomorrow and Linda will need someone to keep her company."

"I'm around," Mason said. "Happy to help."

"I don't need a babysitter." Linda tightened her grip on Sorcha's arm, worried she'd trip and take them both down.

"That's not what I said or implied," Mason said.

Linda knew that was true, but she didn't want to feel indebted to him. It may have seemed like he came to her rescue, but she could have handled the situation on her own. She'd been calculating the effectiveness of a swift knee kick when Mason had grabbed Smarmy.

Besides, she could see right through Sorcha's comments. Her goal was to get something started between Linda and Mason. But they'd been down that road before—twice—and it hadn't worked out. She wasn't trying for number three.

Mason was thankful the sky was cloudy, and the moon's light was dull. He caught Sorcha's meaning, and it made him smile. But he sensed, more than saw, Linda stiffen. Even after six years apart, he was perfectly in tune with

Linda's body language. She didn't want to rely on him. And she didn't like her friend goading her on.

While he didn't want to be seen as searching her out, he was thankful he'd been in the bar when that jerk got in her face. As soon as the man had approached Linda and her roommate, Mason had gone on high alert. He'd instinctively stood and started walking slowly around the bar, ready to spring into action if needed.

When the menace got in Linda's face, Mason saw red, and his body moved without his mind's permission. He lunged.

As mad as he was about the guy's actions, Mason was more irritated that he could no longer watch Linda and her friend laugh and enjoy themselves. They'd been loose and having a great time.

The sight of them dancing made him think about the house party he and Linda had gone to just before they broke up. Scratch that. Just before Mason took off and left Linda with a lot of questions and no answers.

It had been a beautiful spring evening, and his buddy was throwing a kegger off campus. He took Linda, hoping they'd have a good time. At that point, it seemed like he was always putting his foot in his mouth with her, saying the opposite of whatever she wanted to hear.

She'd taken to dancing that night as well, and he'd loved watching her enjoy herself. It'd been a special night, almost magical, until his car got towed and the night was spoiled.

"Can't believe we have to be up in..." Sorcha paused and looked at her phone. She hiccupped loudly and Mason hoped everyone in the condo building had their windows closed. "Four hours. Yikes!" she finished.

They stepped into the doorway, and Mason punched in his entrance code. Before the door closed, Linda punched in her number as well, and Mason wondered why, when the door was already open. Must be out of habit.

At the elevator, Sorcha jabbed at the button. "Why did you let me drink so much?"

"I tried to tell you." Linda shrugged. "I tried to pull you out of there three times."

"You did?"

"Yep."

The elevator doors opened, and Mason waited for the women to enter. Linda went first and faced him as he entered. Her eyes looked tired, and the skin across her shoulders was pink.

"You got some sun today," he observed.

The corner of her mouth raised in a wince. "Beach day, and we went parasailing."

"You did?"

Sorcha swayed forward, and Linda steadied her. "It was a blast!"

The elevator carted them to the fourth floor, and when the doors opened, Mason let them exit first. At the door to his condo, he waited to watch Linda unlock her door. "Good night, you two. Nice to meet you, Sorcha. Have a safe flight."

Sorcha's hand waved as she walked into the condo, calling out her farewell.

Linda paused in the doorway and looked at him. "Thank you. For walking home with us. And for pulling Smarmy off me."

"Of course."

She entered her condo and closed the door behind her. Mason shook his keys, looking for the right one.

Inside, he left the lights off and walked to the fridge to grab a beer. He'd left a full one open on the bar at Crabbie's.

He went to the patio door and slid it open. On the balcony, he eased into a patio chair and took a deep breath, letting the fresh air fill his lungs.

The light from next door flipped on and he knew Linda was in the bedroom. He knew that condo as well as he knew his own. He hoped she'd come outside before going to bed, but she did not. When the light clicked off again, he whispered, "Night, Lindy."

Chapter 6

Linda took Sorcha to the airport for an early Sunday send-off, then returned to the condo for a long nap. Feeling refreshed, she entered the condo building's recreation center at noon to help Meridian facilitate the afternoon's bingo session. Bingo was at two, and the residents would come early for refreshments. The ladies needed to get the tables set up before anyone arrived.

"How many of these are we setting up?" Linda asked, walking backwards with the ten-foot-long table bouncing against her upper legs.

"Six," Meridian responded. She was shorter than Linda, so the table sloped towards her. "It may be more than we need, but I'd rather have too many than not enough."

"Sure."

"Whoa! Stop there," Meri commanded.

Linda stopped, and they leaned over to put the table on its edge before pulling out the squeaky, metal legs.

"Thanks again for volunteering, Linda."

"Not a problem. I don't mind staying out of the sun in the early afternoon."

"Smart girl."

Meri stood up and pushed her dark brunette bangs out of her eyes. She wore a short-sleeved denim top, and Linda wondered if it was as warm as it looked.

They quickly set up the rest of the tables, then Meri got out the bingo supplies, stored in a twenty-gallon plastic tote. The residents were serious about bingo!

The door to the lounge opened, and Linda looked over to see Mason walking in. He was wearing a light blue T-shirt and board shorts with dolphins on them.

The sight of him made Linda's heart flip-flop. She wanted to be indifferent to him. It had been a long time since he'd walked out of her life, and she thought she'd made peace with it. But seeing him was wreaking havoc on her resolve.

His eyes still radiated the warmth and charm that had initially attracted her to him. And his smile made the lucky recipient feel special. How did he still do this to her, after he'd hurt her so badly?

"Hello, ladies!" he called as he entered.

"Mason!" Meri called. He approached and gave her a big hug. "It's been too long since I've seen you."

"I know. Haven't been here for a while. It's good to be back." He looked at Linda, and she felt butterflies in her stomach. She wished they were hangover spasms!

"We'll have to catch up," Meri said, patting his arm. "Hey, did you hear about the Blueberry Festival?"

"No." Mason shook his head. "What's that?"

"A big to-do. We need more volunteers this week, and I was planning to ask Linda today." She turned towards Linda with a plea in her eyes. "But since you're here, I'll ask you both."

"What do volunteers need to do?" Mason asked.

"Many things. But I need two people to sell raffle tickets for the festival and the Saturday night gala. I think the two of you would be perfect!"

Linda shook her head. "Meri, I'm not only on vacation. I have to work a few hours every day."

Meri looked at her quizzically. "What time?"

"It fluctuates, but usually ten to one or noon to three."

Meri smiled. "Not a problem! I need you from seven to ten each morning, Monday to Thursday. Please say yes. I'm desperate. I thought I had a couple of locals lined up, but they called yesterday and backed out. I don't know what I'll do if you two can't help!"

Mason looked at Linda. "I'm game if you are."

Meri held her hands together in front of her chest. "Pretty please!"

Linda rolled her eyes as she smiled back at Meri. "How can I say no to your sweet face?"

"You can't!" Meri clapped and raised her hands overhead in a victory gesture. "I got you now, suckers!"

"What did we get ourselves into?" Linda groaned.

Mason leaned against the wall with his arms crossed. "Now I'm worried!"

Meri laughed again and said, "Now, let's get ready for bingo!"

For the next hour, they helped Meri set up—she did not want to face disappointment or anger from the residents if bingo wasn't ready to go on time.

Meri glanced at her watch. "We're ready with ten minutes to spare. Now let me tell you about the gig."

Linda smiled to herself; Meri made it sound like they were going to be performing. Meri would be sorely mistaken if she thought Linda had any musical or acting talent.

Mr. and Mrs. Sorenson entered the lounge as Meri explained how to sell gala tickets to the Blueberry and Blues Festival. Meri abruptly stopped talking to Linda and Mason and welcomed the residents to bingo.

Mason looked at Linda and shrugged his broad shoulders. "Sounds easy enough."

"Agree." Setting up a table and selling tickets in front of the grocery store would be easy, but sitting next to Mason for three hours every morning might not be.

"Are you staying to help with the bingo game?" Mason asked her.

"Yes. You?"

"No. I'm going for a jog. I saw you two in here and thought I'd stop in. Say hi."

"You underestimated Meri's skill at leveraging able bodies into doing her bidding," Linda said as she waved to Ms. Esquivel, who was walking in, carrying her tiny Pekingese dog under one arm. Poor dog.

"Yes, I did. Hope you don't mind being stuck with me the next few days."

"Anything for Meri." Linda stressed the last word. She wanted it to be clear to Mason that she was doing this for Meri, not to spend time with him.

"Yes, of course," Mason agreed. "Hey, how was Sorcha this morning? Make it to her flight on time?"

"She did. I sort of feel sorry for whoever had to sit next to her. I'm sure it was a rough flight."

Mason laughed. "Well, why don't we go to dinner tonight and catch up?" he asked. He paused and shook the hand of Mr. Green, who'd tapped him on the shoulder. After exchanging pleasantries with the octogenarian, he turned back to Linda. "Then we can make plans to meet up and drive to the location this week."

You mean clear the air. Make it not so awkward. "Fine. We need to coordinate."

"Great. Seven-thirty?"

She nodded.

"I'll knock on your door then. I'll drive."

As always, the jog helped clear Mason's head. The pounding of his feet on the sand and the pounding of the waves hitting the sandy shore helped clear the pounding in his head whenever he remembered the way Linda seemed to tense up whenever he got near her.

He strategized about how to approach dinner as his legs hit their stride and his body ran on autopilot. He would need to address the reasons he'd left. And why he hadn't stayed in contact all these years.

It'd been too much. He'd needed to run emotionally back then, much as he needed to run physically now: to clear his head and gain perspective.

How would Linda understand his need to find himself? She always seemed comfortable in her own skin. Comfortable enough to color her hair pink, or blue, or purple. It had started as a way to distinguish herself from her sister, but she had fully embraced it, and it had become ingrained in her personality.

While the twins might have looked alike, their personalities were so different that Mason had never mixed the two of them up after knowing them for a couple of weeks.

Laurel was no nonsense, a driver. A natural leader. Linda always said Laurel was a bossy big sister. He'd seen the number of times that Laurel had overstepped and been a brat, so he understood Linda's feelings.

Being the baby of the family was something he and Linda had in common. It was probably the main thing that made them close as kids. Laurel and Erin would team up and decide what the four of them would do. Half the time, Linda and Mason would rebel and take off to do their own thing.

A seagull swooped low in front of him and seemed to hover in his face, staying five feet ahead of him as he ran forward.

"What?" he asked the floating bird. "I don't have any food."

The bird launched itself back into the sky.

He would have to apologize to Linda as a start and try to explain to her how emotionally frail he'd been back when they graduated from college. Losing his mom to cancer had been devastating. The pressure from his dad to be a doctor was relentless and unnerving.

Deciding to change his major from pre-med to nursing was the start of Mason's rebellion. Deciding to be a traveling nurse and get the heck out of central Illinois was the icing on the rebellion cupcake.

He'd never wanted to hurt Linda. He'd been the one to ratchet up their relationship when his mom got sick. Linda was supportive and caring and kind to him when he needed it most. It had seemed inevitable to fall for her.

But just when he had geared himself up to tell her he was going to take a position in Atlanta, Georgia to put some distance between himself and his dad and battle his way out from under the funk he'd been under since his mom died, she'd told him she loved him. The timing was awful.

He loved Linda, but he needed time on his own. He knew if he'd stayed and they'd proceeded down the path they were on, they would've been married within a couple of years and had kids a couple of years after that. Then he'd never know if he'd pursued nursing because it was his calling or because he'd chickened out of becoming a doctor.

Once he was married and a dad, he wouldn't know if it had been the right decision or not. He wouldn't have been able to go back to school and become a doctor with a family to provide for.

That's what he'd wanted to tell Linda that night he told her he was taking a position in Atlanta. But she'd blurted out "I love you" at the same time he'd said, "I'm moving" and then chaos broke out.

He'd been mature enough to know that he wasn't ready to settle down, that he had big questions about his future to sort out before he brought a serious relationship or a wife into his messy life. But he wasn't mature enough to tell Linda all of that.

He hurt her, and then he ran. Ran from Illinois, ran from his dad and his sister, ran from Linda—the best thing about his life, then and always.

A cramp gripped his side. He stopped and bent over, trying to control his breath and the pain. Glancing at the watch as his hand dangled between his face and the sand, he saw that he'd been jogging for forty-five minutes. No wonder he'd cramped up.

Chapter 7

"No way!" Linda shrieked into the phone.

"Way! He's hot. You're both there. Alone. Girl, get you some," Sorcha practically purred. Linda had called her to make sure she'd made it home with no issues. She had. Sorcha grilled her about the day, and Linda confessed to dinner plans with Mason.

"I can't get involved with him again." Linda put the phone on speaker so she could use the flat iron on her hair. "Told you. We tried it before. It would be too weird."

"Come on. How weird can it be? He lives out of a suitcase and seems to be allergic to Illinois. It may be another six years before you see him again."

True. A heaviness lay on Linda's heart. Even though Mason had said he was tired of moving so much, until he stopped, she would never be sure. Linda shook her head, knowing Sorcha couldn't see her. "I'm glad you're home. I need to let you go so I can finish getting ready."

"All right, but if you hook up, you have to call me when you get in. If you don't call tonight, I'll know you hooked up."

"You're going to crash tonight. We were out late last night, and you traveled today. I'm not calling you. Besides, I'm not hooking up with him. That's impossible."

Sorcha laughed. "Nothing's impossible, Lulu. You gotta believe!"

Linda rolled her eyes and hung up. Her roommate was that blessed mix of sass and spunk that kept Linda on her toes.

Twenty minutes later, her hair was done, her makeup was applied, and her nerves were jumping when a knock sounded at the door. She froze in place and took a deep breath. *It's only Mason.*

Counting out each step as her feet made their way to the door, she glanced toward the wall of windows facing the Gulf and exhaled, the sight of the blue sky and pink streaks in the clouds calming her down.

"Hi," she said, opening the door.

Mason had recently showered; his hair was damp, and the top curled slightly. He wore a dark blue polo shirt and tan cargo shorts. Linda worried she had overdressed in her strapless sundress. She wanted to look nice, not for Mason's sake, but for her own.

Mason whistled, and Linda felt her cheeks warm.

"You look amazing. As always," Mason said. "Ready to go?"

"Thank you," she demurred. "I am."

She grabbed her purse and followed him out the door.

Mason led the way to the elevator. "Do you have a problem if we drive a little way for dinner? It's such a beautiful evening. I thought a ride in the convertible along the coast was in order."

So much for straightening my hair. "That sounds great. I love your dad's convertible. Erin took me for a ride when we were here last fall."

Mason cut a glance towards her. "Yeah, it's great."

Linda wondered what the look was for. Had Erin not told him that the girls had come for a getaway? Had she told him something else?

"How's Erin doing?" Linda didn't want to pry, but it seemed like neutral territory.

The elevator door finally opened. "She's fine. We spoke briefly last week. She was at work."

"Laurel says Erin works too hard and is always exhausted." Linda fidgeted with the clasp on her purse; it didn't want to stay closed when she tucked it under her arm. "Laurel asked Erin to promise her she'd take off the two days leading up to her wedding, so she doesn't fall asleep during the ceremony."

Mason rolled his shoulders as he leaned against the wall on the side of the elevator, next to the buttons. "Sounds about right. Erin has a hard time turning down extra shifts at the hospital. I think it's because of the ridiculous amount she owes on her student loans. She says she won't get married or start a family with all her debt. I'm thankful that I was able to tackle mine head on."

The elevator bumped to a stop, and Mason motioned for her to lead. They were in the underground parking garage, and Linda walked towards Mr. Hauser's convertible. It was a cherry-red two-seater Audi TT. It was a gorgeous vehicle and a lot of fun to ride in. Linda had laughed when she'd first seen Mr. Hauser in it. He had shrugged and said it was the prerequisite midlife-mobile. He said losing his beautiful wife had made him realize life was short, and he wanted to spend more time on enjoying the "little things"—like little red sports cars.

Underway, Linda asked where they were going, but Mason was elusive. Once they were driving along the coast and the air was filling her lungs and making a mess of her hair, she decided she didn't care where they were going or about her hair. She was going to relax and enjoy the evening. She would focus on the fact that Mason was a childhood friend, not simply an ex-boyfriend who flew the coop.

Twenty minutes later they arrived at Midcoast Inn, a family-friendly seafood restaurant that was built on piers over the Gulf. It had been a favorite place for the families to go when they wanted to get away from the condo and the handful of restaurants in Seaside Bay.

"Wow, I haven't been here in years," Linda said, stepping out of the car.

"Oh, yeah? I try to come every time I'm here. They have the best clam chowder. I've tried it everywhere, from Maine to Oregon, and there is no comparison."

"I remember when you refused to try it when we were kids."

"Yes, Mom thought I would never try. But I finally gave in."

"You've always been stubborn."

"Maybe." He shrugged as he opened the door.

Inside the restaurant, Linda glanced at the wooden walls, the fishing nets draped about the room, and the seagull decor everywhere.

Mason asked the receptionist for a table on the outside deck. Seated, Linda looked in her purse for lip balm. Her lips were dry from the wind whipping through the car.

They ordered, and once the waitress brought their drinks, Mason raised his for a toast.

"To reconnecting," he said.

"To reconnecting and volunteering for Meri," Linda replied, to remind Mason why they were there.

"Right. Let's get down to tactics, then we can move on to fun stuff. It's a twenty-minute drive to the grocery store, and we need to be there at seven." He paused and glanced at his watch. "Why don't I knock on your door at six?"

An hour before we have to be there? Is he joking?
"Seriously? That early?"

"Well, we have to set up the table and make sure we're ready to go at seven."

"How are we getting the table there in your dad's convertible?"

"Meri said there's a table there that the store will let us use. We need to ask them to get it out of their break room."

"Oh, good. I still don't know that we need that much time."

"I hate to be late." He smiled and raised his eyebrows.

The rays from the setting sun brought out a soft red undertone in his hair color that she didn't remember being there. Funny what six years did to your memory of someone you'd loved.

She relented. "Fine. Six is fine."

Planning the early morning start made Linda appreciate working from home even more. She normally rolled out of bed five minutes before she needed to be online for work.

"Great!" He leaned forward and Linda felt herself bracing. "Now. I think we need to do something a little outrageous to get people's attention at 7 a.m."

"Outrageous?"

"Yes, we need music or costumes. Something to lure the shoppers to us so we can sell tickets. I want to knock Meri's socks off with our success."

"You know this is a volunteer gig, right?"

"Sure. But that doesn't mean we slack off. We should always give a hundred percent."

"I didn't suggest slacking. I just don't know about costumes. How are we going to pull that off in—" She glanced at the time on her phone. "Ten hours?"

"Good point. Tomorrow will be tough. We need to use what's on hand. Let me think." He leaned back, and Linda could tell his foot was tapping from the way his body jiggled.

"I didn't pack any costumes." Linda took a sip of her diet cola and looked at the water. The sun would set soon, and she worried it would be chilly sitting outside. She should have grabbed a sweater for her bare arms.

"Wouldn't expect you to. Maybe we each have something that matches. It's a blueberry festival. What do you have that's dark blue?"

"A pair of jeans?"

"Denim. We can work with that. What about a solid blue shirt? Light blue, medium...whatever."

"Um, no."

"Well, a plain T-shirt is easy to find. We can stop and find one on our way back tonight. Tomorrow, we'll wear blue jeans and a blue T-shirt. We'll coordinate. Now, let's brainstorm ideas for the rest of the week. We could be blueberry farmers, or blues musicians..."

Linda shook her head. "You're crazy."

"No, the idea might be crazy, but I'm not. I'm perfectly normal."

She raised an eyebrow. "Are you now?"

"Well..." Mason laughed, that deep, throaty laugh that used to make her toes curl. She glanced down at her feet in the tan sandals. They were curling. *Dang it!*

"Whatever you come up with, how are we going to find outfits?"

"The thrift store! We could let that be our inspiration. Let's go shopping tomorrow afternoon and see what we come up with. It'll be a hoot."

This is why Linda had loved being around Mason. He was always full of adventure. He never met a stranger or ran from a challenge. Well, except for when he ran from her, when she'd put her heart on the line. The thought took the smile away from her face, and she felt as if someone had punched her in the gut.

"Hey," Mason leaned towards her and tapped her hand. "Where'd you go there? Don't tell me you're too good for a thrift store."

"I love thrifting. It's not that, I...guess I'm getting hungry." It was a lame excuse, but she hoped he'd accept it.

"I am, too. What do you say? Thrift tomorrow afternoon?"

"I need to work a few hours midday. Maybe we could go around three?"

"That sounds perfect. Ah!" He looked past her. "Here comes our food."

The waitress set down Linda's seafood Alfredo and Mason's grilled sea bass. "Can I get you anything else?"

Mason looked at her, his eyes wide, waiting. She shook her head, and he glanced at the waitress. "We're good for now."

"Do we have a solid enough plan for this week that we can talk about something else?" Linda asked, twirling pasta around her fork.

"Yes, for now. What do you want to talk about next?" Mason spritzed lemon juice across his fish.

"Tell me about work. How is it, starting a new gig every few months and having to pick up and move?"

Linda had been curious about this for a long time. She couldn't imagine the stress of starting over so often. New city, new apartment, new coworkers. It was a lot of new, and she liked her routine.

"It's fun. Challenging but fun. I feel energized by the movement. Packing up and moving on is a great way to pause, reflect, and prep for something new."

"Think you'll do this for your entire career?" She braced herself for his answer.

Mason looked down quickly and smoothed the napkin on his lap. "No. As fun as it is, I've been thinking it's time to settle into one place. But I'm trying to figure out where. I've lived in some amazing places. Chicago is fantastic. Full of interesting architecture, things to do. I loved San Diego. The weather is amazing, though the sun can be a little intense. Maybe I could settle somewhere new for a while. Maybe a smaller city like Des Moines or Indianapolis. Little closer to Dad and my sister."

Me! Linda felt shocked when the word suddenly popped into her mind, demanding attention. "Why not Peoria or Bloomington? If you want to be closer to your family..."

"I don't know. I feel like I've been running from home for so long, I'm not sure I can go back. You know?"

"No. I don't know. I've always lived within a sixty-mile radius of where I was born. Never lived anywhere else. I've only vacationed outside of Illinois."

"That's cool, too. If that's what you want. I've always wanted to see everything. Experience everything. Thought about moving to Europe, but it seemed like too much of a hassle. I've got a good process down here. Find an apartment or extended-stay hotel within one mile of the hospital I'll be working at, so I don't need a car. I can pack or unpack within sixty minutes. When I arrive someplace new, I take a day to study the lay of the land. Bus schedules, train schedules, restaurants, grocery stores. Then I throw myself into work. Taking extra shifts. Figuring out how I can make an impact while I'm there, and then I do what I love. Work for the patients, making sure they're comfortable, stable, and healing."

"You love nursing." Linda took a bite of her heavenly Alfredo.

"I do. Funny how life turns out. Until Mom got sick, I had never considered it. Figured I would follow Dad's path and become a doctor, like Erin. But nursing is the thing for me. It's my calling."

"I think it's great that you found your calling. I'm still searching for mine."

"Do you like what you're doing?"

"I do. I love working for Grady. He's the best!"

Mason's forehead pinched together. Linda ignored it.

"The work is interesting," she continued. "I like problem solving, making sure things get done on time, making sure Grady's real estate empire is growing."

"Grady?" Mason asked. "Sounds like you're close."

"Sure. We've been close. He's a good friend, a great boss. But I don't know if it's what I want to do for the rest of my life. I have a side hustle, and I enjoy the creativity I get to put into it. And I enjoy knowing I'm one hundred percent responsible for the success or failure of my business."

"What's your side hustle?" Mason took another roll out of the breadbasket and buttered it.

"I make printables and sell them on Etsy. Like party invitations, budget spreadsheets, packing lists, that sort of thing."

Mason was nodding. "That's mighty! Mighty nice."

She took a bite of creamy goodness. "Thanks. I think so. It's taken a while for me to find my niche. I'd like to expand it, but I don't want to expand too soon. Or take on more than I can handle."

"I can't imagine that happening. You're a rock star, Lindy!"

"You don't know that. I feel like I'm barely keeping it together some days."

Why did I tell him that?

Mason shook his head. "We all have bad days, but you focus on the good days. I'm sure nine out of ten times you have everything under control."

She blushed. She did. That's why Grady was always praising her work ethic. She didn't like to take risks. Except with hair color. Or clothing choices. But never with Grady's business or her own.

Why was sitting here, eating dinner with Mason, feeling like a risk? Her inner alert system was suddenly in overdrive. She couldn't let his charm and enthusiasm win her over again. He would move on soon. He always did. She would not let her heart get wrapped up in his orbit again. Falling to earth and crash-landing after he moved on was too painful.

"How long are you here for before you go to your next town?" she asked.

"Two weeks."

There you have it. "Huh. We'll be leaving here about the same time. I fly home on the fourteenth."

"I will likely leave on the thirteenth."

"Likely?"

"It depends on where I go next. I haven't decided."

That's the thing—Mason couldn't decide. It was between Seattle, Washington and Portland, Maine. Which northern coastal town was calling him the loudest? He wasn't above flipping a coin, and he might have to do that with this decision.

Linda's gaze dropped, but not before he saw the turbulence in her eyes. If he didn't know better, he would say she was upset. Whether because he wasn't coming back to Illinois or for something else, he wasn't sure.

She mumbled something, and he leaned forward. "I'm sorry?"

"Nothing." She looked up and smiled, but it seemed forced. "Where might you go?"

"Seattle or Portland. Portland, Maine, not Oregon. I've lived there before, so I want to go somewhere new."

"Wow. I've always wanted to see Seattle."

"You've never been?"

"No."

"Well, maybe that's where I should go then. Then you'd have an excuse to visit. And a place to stay." He groaned internally. Why did he throw that out there?

She started to speak but shook her head like she changed her mind about something. "I hear Maine is beautiful."

"It is. I took a weekend trip there when I lived in Boston."

He saw her shiver. "Hey, it's getting cold. I have a sweatshirt in the car. Let me run and get it for you."

"You don't need to do that. I'm fine," she protested.

"Nope. Be right back."

He jumped up and hurried back through the restaurant. He had to slow to get around a man in a walker, being prodded along by his purple-haired wife. Mason smiled to see the woman's hair; he could imagine Linda with that bright purple color.

Outside, he dashed to the car and popped the trunk. He was thankful he'd tossed the New York Mets sweatshirt in there earlier. He'd bought it for warmth the previous summer when a mid-July game had turned unseasonably cool.

Back at their table, he handed the sweatshirt to Linda. Her shoulders dropped, and she thanked him before pulling it on. She looked tiny in his shirt.

"Glad it was in the car. It should keep you warm," he said. Looking at his plate, he realized the rest of the entrée would be too cold to eat now. He tossed his napkin over it.

He noticed Linda had finished eating as well. "Would you like dessert?"

She gave him a half-smile. "Does a bear sleep in the woods?"

"That's the Linda I know. Always up for dessert."

"Always. There is a raspberry cheesecake on the menu that sounds divine."

"Ah, you studied that part of the menu, did you?"

"I start with dessert, then plan my meal."

"Smart lady. Now, tell me about your parasailing expedition. I want to know more. I've never been."

The waitress swung by, removing plates, and taking dessert orders. Linda gushed about parasailing with her roommate. He studied her while she spoke. He'd hoped to rekindle their friendship, but if he was honest with himself, he'd gladly rekindle more.

He'd wanted to explain why he'd broken up with her and left after college, but now that they were here, he couldn't. It felt like they were on a boat at sea rather than on a dock next to the Gulf. Things were too rocky to broach the subject now. He needed to reestablish some trust and camaraderie with Linda before bringing up the past. They would spend hours together this week volunteering for Meri. He hoped by the end of the week they would be in a better place for the long-overdue conversation.

Chapter 8

Linda rubbed her eyes as she opened the door.

"Morning, Sunshine!" Mason was too chipper. "Here, I brought you a cappuccino. Vanilla this time. If you don't like it, I can make you something else."

She took the cup he offered and brought it to her nose, inhaling deeply. "Need." She took a sip and sighed. "This is perfect. Thank you."

Mason laughed. "I have replenishments." He held up a green thermos bottle.

"Good."

"Ready?"

"I suppose."

Linda followed him down the hall, appreciating his lack of conversation, which continued during the drive. While he didn't chit-chat, he whistled, which was almost as annoying, but Linda held her tongue. She worried if he wasn't whistling, he'd want to talk, and it was too early and too "BC"—before coffee—for that.

Once they had the table set up and had taken out their supplies, which Mason had brought in a back-pack—gala tickets, a money box, a Bluetooth speaker, festival flyers, and a small notebook and pen—Linda asked for the thermos to refill her coffee cup.

"I'm ready for a refill as well," Mason said, sitting in the folding chair the grocery store had provided them.

Linda took the lid off the Tampa Bay Rays mug that Mason had brought her. Mason said hello to a customer exiting the store. The man shook his head when Mason suggested the gala ticket.

"This is going to be fun," Mason said, holding his cup out for a refill.

"Says you." Linda filled his cup.

"I hope we sell lots of tickets for Meri."

"I do, too."

After filling the mugs, Linda took out her phone and pulled up her to-do list. Grady had a couple of important projects going on this week that Linda needed to keep an eye on. First up was a bid on an abandoned property that Grady's girlfriend, Nica, wanted. Grady said it would be a great opportunity. With summer coming, Nica wanted to rehab the property while she was on school break. Linda needed to complete a project proposal for Grady's investors by Wednesday. She needed a few hours today to work on it, then she could polish it on Tuesday and get it in on time.

Grady also asked that she follow up on several delinquent tenants and complete five lease extensions by Friday. Maybe this wasn't the best week to work remotely. She probably needed a couple of full-time workdays, and volunteering with Mason was putting pressure on her time.

"I'm thinking about adopting a python. What do you think?" Mason said.

"What the what?" Linda's head jerked around.

Mason chuckled. "Got your attention. Just kidding. Could you imagine me flying with a snake? What would other passengers think?"

"I think it would have to go in the cargo hold, not in the cabin."

"You sure about that? You see people with dogs and cats in the cabin."

"Not sure how I feel about that. I would worry about people with allergies sitting next to me if I brought my cats."

"You have cats? Multiple?"

A woman carrying a toddler boy on her hip approached and Mason stood. "Hello, Miss. We're selling tickets to this weekend's Blueberry and Blues Festival. We have general admission tickets and tickets to the gala on Saturday night. Which can I get for you?"

Linda admired his confidence. Mason had always been friendly and outgoing. He was the life of the party and the center of attention wherever they went. It was comforting to be in his orbit. It seemed to be no effort for him, and it took the pressure off her to be "on".

"Oh, yes!" the woman responded. "We need two adult tickets. General ones. Can't afford the gala."

"Coming right up!" Mason leaned down to tear off two tickets from the booklet. "That will be twenty dollars."

The woman paid him and hurried away.

Mason placed the money in the metal box and sat back down. "Cats?" he prompted.

"Yes. Two cats. Missy and Buddy."

"What kind?"

"Run of the mill, domestic shorthair cats. Want to see a picture?" Linda flipped over to the gallery on her phone and pulled up a picture of the gray siblings.

"How do you tell them apart? They look alike!"

"Buddy has a small patch of white on his chest. You can't see it in this picture. Hold on." She thumbed through the pictures until she found one of Buddy sitting regally, eyes half-closed, looking at the camera.

"Ah. I see. Who watched them while you and Sorcha were here?"

"They are staying with Laurel." Linda laid her phone on the table. "She says she likes cat sitting. She can enjoy them for a while and then send them home."

"That works out. Is Laurel still in Peoria?"

"Yes. She's doing well. She's in line for the principal position at her school. If she gets it this fall, she'll be the youngest principal the school has ever had."

"Doesn't surprise me," Mason enthused. "She has always been good about going after what she wants."

Linda looked away. It was like Mason stuck a needle under her fingernail. Comparisons to Laurel always caused her to stiffen up. She felt "less than" when compared to her twin. Laurel excelled at everything she did and went after what she wanted.

Linda sighed and responded. "That she is." Trying to shift the conversation, she said, "So, tell me more about your life on the run." Hmm, that was truer than she'd intended. "I bet you have a girlfriend in every port." *Bet he left a girlfriend in every port.*

"Oh, we're going there, are we? I assumed dating was an off-limits topic. But I'm glad you brought it up. I have questions myself." He turned to face her squarely. "To start with, no, I don't have a girlfriend in *any* port. When you put down roots for only twelve weeks at a time, it's hard to see anyone long enough."

"Oh? So, you're telling me you haven't dated in six years?"

"I didn't say that. I've dated. Here and there. But I keep things casual. Knowing I'll be moving on. So, no girlfriends scattered across the U.S." He reached over and nudged her shoulder. "How about you? How many hearts have you broken since I saw you last?"

Did he forget he broke mine? Glibly, she replied, "Oh, dozens. Love 'em and leave 'em, I always say."

"Hey, you're not being honest with me. I thought we could be honest with each other. I hope we can be friends again."

"Friends again?"

"Yes. I've missed you, Lindy! I know I botched everything when I left after college. I can't tell you how many times I've lamented my actions..."

A man in a three-piece suit approached them. Mason must have seen him out of the corner of his eye, because he groaned and stood. He greeted the man and pitched festival tickets. The man said he was only in town for a couple of days and would be gone before the weekend. He looked at Linda and winked at her. "Wish I was staying," he said, before hustling into the store.

"Dang!" Mason shook his head. "I can't believe he outright flirted with you in front of me."

"It's not like we're wearing a sign that suggests we're together."

"We're sitting here together. We're both wearing blue T-shirts."

"Get real. We probably look more like siblings than a couple."

"I hope you're wrong about that."

Linda was glad the interruption had changed the trajectory of the conversation. She didn't want to discuss relationships with Mason. Maybe they should just stick to the task at hand. Maybe she could pretend Mason was her brother and put the whole idea of relationships out of her head.

Yuck. She'd kissed Mason. Lots of times. She could not think of him as a brother.

"Meri said she was impressed that we sold forty tickets to the festival and fourteen to the gala."

"Great! I'm here to make Meri merry."

"Ha!" Mason replied. They were in their first thrift store of the afternoon. After their volunteer stint in the morning, they'd gone back to their respective condos so Linda could work.

She'd spent a few hours working on the property proposal and was ready to get outside when Mason called to check on her.

Now they were in Second Time's the Charm, a thrift store a few miles from Seaside Bay that she'd found with Laurel and Erin the previous fall. They talked to the owner, who was a lady in her late thirties who spent hours outside smoking when no one was in the store.

"Oh, what about this?" Linda pulled a large pink poodle skirt off the rack. "A poodle skirt. We could do a rockabilly theme!"

"Yes!" Mason pumped a fist in the air, his biceps flexed, and Linda gulped. "I could roll up my jeans, put on a white tee, and slick back my hair. That would be easy."

"Uh, huh," she murmured, still thinking about his biceps. Think! "I need a white blouse and something I can tie around my neck."

"You'll need short socks and black shoes."

"Ok. That's one era of music. What else are you thinking?" They'd wear music-related costumes if they could pull it off.

"Hey, look." Mason pointed, and Linda found her eyes still lingering on his arm. "There's a *Blues Brothers* movie poster. Maybe we could find black suits and do that."

"Good thing we have morning shifts. It would get too hot to wear a black suit in the afternoon."

"True. But our seats are in shade, so it won't be too hot."

"Right."

They continued browsing the racks. Mason quickly found an appropriate black suit, but it took more digging for Linda to find a similar suit that would work for *The Blues Brothers* duo.

"Hey, Lindy!" Mason called, and Linda glanced up from the slinky green dress she was holding, wondering if it would work for a genre of music. She giggled as she saw Mason. He was wearing a large yellow hat with a gigantic parrot on top of it. "We could be parrot-heads. You know,

Jimmy Buffett. He's a music style all his own, and very apropos for Florida. We can do this."

"Hawaiian shirts, khaki shorts, and flip-flops. Yes, we could do that easily. Are you seriously thinking about getting that hat?"

"It's a done deal. The hat is mine." His eyebrows pinched in concentration. "Would I need a separate carry-on to take this hat with me when I travel?"

"Just wear it. You'd be the life of the party. As usual."

He was the life of the party. His spirit was infectious, always quick with a joke. That's what had always attracted her to him. He was like quicksand. If you got too close, you'd be sucked in and unable to get out. She couldn't have that. She turned back to the dress in her hand. Shaking her head, she hung it back up.

She needed to put herself in check. If she wasn't careful, she would fall back in love with Mason just in time for him to take off again. Why was she attracted to the men she couldn't have? The only good thing about being attracted to unavailable men was that if she remembered to keep her wits and not fall for them, she wouldn't get hurt.

It was like she'd been infected with the Mason virus. Sort of like shingles, it lurked deep inside her body, a time bomb, ticking to pop out when she least expected it. Similar to every third date she had with a guy. The first date was exciting, getting to know someone new, and seeing if they were compatible. The second date was optimistic. They'd made it past the first one. There was mutual interest. But by the third date, it was always apparent that this person wasn't Mason. Linda rarely made it to a fourth date.

"Ugh," she moaned softly. She needed a date for Laurel's wedding in two months. She might have to resort to a dating app to find someone. Working from home made it impossible to meet new people, and she hated meeting someone at a bar. In her experience, meeting someone while drinking had never led to a successful first date, so she'd stopped trying.

"What's wrong?" Mason was next to her, leaning down to look her in the eyes.

She hadn't noticed Mason approach. "Huh?"

"You groaned. What's wrong?" Worry lines creased his forehead. Linda wanted to reach up and smooth them, but she kept her hands at her sides.

"Nothing. Just remembering something else I need to do."

"Are you going to write it down on your phone, so you don't forget?" He nodded towards the purse hanging across her body.

"When did you..."

"You are always jotting notes down. You did it half a dozen times this morning."

"Didn't realize you noticed that."

He shrugged. "I notice everything. Goes with the job. Don't be embarrassed. Go ahead and write it down. We need to move on to another thrift store. I can't find any-thing else. I'll pay for our stuff while you jot-jot."

He reached for the suit and the skirt in her hand. "I can pay for my stuff," she protested.

"I know you can, but I roped you into doing this. Let me get it."

He had roped her in. She handed him the garments and pulled out her phone.

She followed him towards the register and listened as the owner flirted with Mason. Linda rolled her eyes. Was there any female over eighteen that didn't drool over him?

The woman touched Mason's arm. Linda's eyes nar-rowed.

"I'll meet you outside," Linda said, tapping Mason on the shoulder.

"Is your wifey mad?" The woman tittered.

"She's, uh..." Mason paused. "Needing some air."

Why didn't he clarify they weren't married? Linda walked out the door and listened to the bell jingle. It was as grating as the woman's laugh.

Chapter 9

Tuesday afternoon, Mason got off the elevator on the first floor while Linda continued onto the fourth.

He wanted to chat with Meri before getting out of his rockabilly gear.

He'd been thrilled when a customer agreed to take a picture of him and Linda at the supermarket. Linda had looked adorable in her poodle skirt, white blouse, white socks, and black shoes. She'd pulled her hair up into a high ponytail and accessorized with all things pink, which matched her hair perfectly. He loved the enthusiasm she'd shown while shopping. He hadn't been sure if she'd go along with it but was thrilled when she had.

He was going to have pictures of them taken together every day while he was here. The pictures would sustain him when he was in the next new town, lonely and homesick.

Yes, he talked a good game, saying he wanted to experience the excitement of a new city every quarter. But staying busy and moving frequently kept the loneliness at bay.

He had hoped the time here, alone, with no timecard to clock and no errands to run, would help him assess where he was in life and where he was going.

The constant moving was growing old, and he was ready to put down real roots. Maybe put in the time and effort to advance his career. That would make his dad happy.

Once he'd discovered that Linda was here, his focus changed. He didn't want to be alone; he wanted to be with her. He was grateful when Linda agreed to volunteer with him to help Meri out.

It'd been a mistake to think he was over her. How could he be? She was the grape jelly to his peanut butter. The milk to his cookie. *Ugh! She's got my mind a mess.*

Meri was in her office when Mason knocked. She looked up from the spiral notebook she was writing in and exclaimed, "Elvis!"

Mason chuckled. "If only I was half as handsome as Elvis. Like the rockabilly look? Look at this picture of Linda and me at the store this morning."

"Love it! Dang!" Meri whistled. "You two have always been the cutest couple."

"We're not a—"

"Gosh, I remember one of the first years your families were down here for Halloween. You and Linda dressed up as Batman and Robin. You were adorable."

"Yeah, I remember that. More from the pictures than an actual memory. Why in the world was she Robin?"

"Linda wanted to do whatever you were doing. Whatever you said, she went along with."

"Maybe when we were nine."

"Okay, things like that don't last forever. Wouldn't hurt you to listen to her more."

Mason plopped into the seat across from Meri. "It may look like everything's fine between us, Meri, but until four days ago, we hadn't spoken in six years." *Give or take two months.*

"No! That's ridiculous!" Meri pulled open a drawer and pulled out a basket of mini chocolate bars. She grabbed a small Twix and yanked off the wrapper. "Help yourself."

Mason waved his hand. "No, thanks. It's true. Before this weekend, the last time we were together, we were dating. Linda was ready to commit to a more serious relationship, and I wanted to move. I needed to get away. My head was still in a messed-up place after losing Mom. I felt like Dad and Erin bounced back too quickly. I tried to talk to Dad about how I was feeling, and he just gave platitudes, like 'your mom's in a better place' and 'Mom wouldn't want you moping, live your life!' It was too much to take."

Meri had been listening quietly—well, as quietly as devouring three mini-Twix bars could be. "That blows. Sorry your dad couldn't be more supportive when you needed him. We can all be a little crappy at how we handle loss. Some people seem to bounce back, as you say, but deep down they're miserable, too. You never know."

She put the chocolate basket back in its drawer. "Now, back to you and Linda. That's it? You took off and broke up? No contact?"

"Yeah." Mason looked at his hands. He needed to trim his nails. "I didn't know how to deal with it. I thought I would call her after I got settled, but once I got settled, it seemed like it was too late."

"It's never too late, son." Meri leaned back in her chair and ran her hands through her brown and gray hair. "Maybe serendipity brought you both here at the same time for a reason. Maybe this is your second chance."

"It would be our third chance."

"Second, third, whatever. You're not out of chances, is my point. Now, I should get back to work. Mr. Peters asked me to plan a May Day party. What's a May Day party?"

"A party that happens on May first?"

"Get out of here, smarty-pants."

Mason smiled and left. In the elevator, he thought about Meri's words. Was it too soon to even contemplate a third chance with Linda? Probably, but when had Mason ever done something expected of him?

As he stepped out of the elevator, the community board across the hall caught his eye. On a yellow sheet of paper was the image of a large fire. Underneath were the words, "Bonfire. Tonight at dusk."

Hmm, that sounds fun. Instead of going to his own condo, he went right to Linda's and knocked.

When she opened the door, he felt disappointment wash over him as he realized she'd changed out of the fifties costume. She still looked good in the pink tank top and long loose shorts with flamingos on them.

"Are those your mom's shorts?" he asked.

"Most likely. Found them in a drawer. What's up?"

"Can I come in? Haven't been in here for ages."

"Fine." She stepped aside, and he entered the condo. It was mostly how he remembered it. Light yellow walls, white couches, and black iron details in the ceiling fixtures and side tables.

He could tell Linda was working at the kitchen table. A laptop was open, and a notebook lay beside it. Even from this distance, he could see a nicely labeled to-do list on the notebook, with several thin strips of floral tape on the edges.

He glanced at the refrigerator, which had a large white paper taped to it. "What's this?" he asked as he stepped closer.

Linda dashed around him and pulled it down, but not before he saw the label at the top. "Requirements for Linda's Date to Laurel's Wedding".

"It's nothing!" Linda choked out. "Just something to humor Sorcha."

Mason smiled at her. "It looked like something I would be interested in reading. Maybe I could help you find a date."

"That's suspect." Linda rolled her eyes. "Who do you even know in Illinois? Do you stay connected to high school or college buddies?"

"A few. Come on. Let me see what's on your list."

"Absolutely not. It's not even accurate. Just stuff I let Sorcha write down." She walked to the trash can and tossed it in. "Now, why did you stop by? You haven't even changed yet?"

"I'm on my way to do that. But I wondered if you saw the sign about the bonfire tonight. Sounds fun. Live music. We can take some beverages."

"A bonfire? No, I didn't see it. I, um. We need to be up early tomorrow."

"Right. We can take seltzer waters or hot cocoa; we don't have to drink alcohol."

"True. If we don't stay out too late, that would be fun." A loud ding sound came from her computer. "Hey, I need to get on a call with my boss to go over a proposal. Gotta run."

"Sure. I know you're working. I'll get out of your hair. The sign said music starts at eight. Want to get dinner before?"

She looked away. "No, I must get this project wrapped up today. Let's plan for eight."

"I'll come and get you then. Later, Lindy."

She walked to the table, and he let himself out.

He paused in the hallway. His chest tightened thinking about how quickly Linda rushed him out the door when her computer pinged, reminding her she needed to talk to her boss. She said her boss had a girlfriend, and she didn't appear to have a thing for the man, but Mason couldn't help the jealousy that tensed his muscles. He needed to go for a run to release the adrenaline coursing through him.

Linda grabbed a hoodie out of the closet. Once the sun went down, she expected it to cool off, even close to the bonfire, and her T-shirt that read "Bayside Bay is Where I Play" would not keep her warm enough.

Waiting for Mason to knock, she took a moment to straighten the living room. She folded the yellow plaid throw blanket, putting it in the wicker basket in the corner, and removed an empty glass from the coffee table.

When the knock sounded at the door, she nearly jumped; she was standing right next to it. She threw it open and laughed at Mason when she saw him standing there with an overstuffed laundry basket.

"What's all this?" she asked.

"I dug through the closets and cabinets in the condo and got everything we could possibly need right here. A beach blanket, thermos of decaf coffee, cups, some packets you toss into a fire to add bright colors, a Polaroid camera, and extra clothes in case it gets cold. And I ran to Franki's Sundries to get s'more fixings and other snacks. Can we go? This is heavy." He lifted the basket and flexed his biceps.

"Wow. You are prepared. I can't remember. Were you a Boy Scout?"

"A few years. I dropped out when my troop stopped doing the pinewood derby. I loved building those cars."

Linda grabbed her hoodie and tossed it into Mason's basket with a wink.

"Hey now!" He laughed. "Are you taking advantage of my muscles?"

Mason flexed as he lifted the basket a few inches.

"Muscles?" Her face flushed and she dipped her head. "I didn't notice. Let's go, Wimpy."

She scooted past him and hurried towards the elevator.

Once Mason caught up with her, she pushed the button and glanced across the hall, seeing the bonfire flyer. "I missed that earlier. Glad you noticed it. Should be fun."

"Agreed." Mason swung the basket from side to side. "Meri's doing a lot of cool new things to add fun and life to the place."

Outside, they strolled over to where Meri was supervising a man preparing the bonfire. There was an enormous pile of logs tented towards the middle. It was going to be a roaring fire.

Mason pointed with his shoulder to the southern side of the bonfire. "Let's go over there. We'll get a splendid view of the sunset."

He led the way and found an open spot. After putting the basket down, he reached in for an extra-large beach blanket. He gave it a flip and arranged it on the sand.

Linda pulled off her flip-flops and walked to the center of the blanket. "What can I do to help set up?"

"Nothing. Just sit."

Meri came over and joked with Mason about his laundry basket.

"Function over form." Mason called to her back as she moved on to Mr. and Mrs. McNett from 3B, right below Mason's family's unit.

Sitting on the blanket, Mason pulled the thermos out. "Decaf?"

"Sure. Nice touch. Coffee sounds better than water or seltzer."

As Mason poured coffee into a mug that read, "Caf or No Caf, That is the Question," a lanky man wearing a funky, dark green cowboy hat began tuning a guitar. He was on the west side of the bonfire, closer to the water.

"How did work go today? Get done what you needed?" Mason asked, handing her a cup.

"Mostly," she answered. "I'm waiting for an estimate from one of our suppliers, which should be in my inbox in the morning, and then I'll get the proposal sent off. Tomorrow is a hard deadline. If I miss it, my boss will kill me."

She put both hands around the mug and brought it closer to her nose. She could smell a hint of cinnamon and a strong whiff of vanilla. "Mm, smells wonderful."

"Thanks. I love tinkering with new blends and flavors."

Linda wiggled, trying to find a comfortable place in the sand.

The musician played a Neil Young tune, and Linda closed her eyes. The warmth of the fire to her right, the heat from Mason's body on her left, and the coffee aroma under her nose filled her with a much-needed sense of peace. She remembered many nights with her family and Mason's family building their own bonfires on this beach. The moms would bring oodles of snacks, and the dads would lead games as they sat around the fire in a circle.

"Do you remember—" Linda started. At the same time Mason said, "Hey, I remember..."

They both laughed, and Mason leaned over to bump her shoulder with his. "Ladies first."

Linda took a sip of coffee and leaned back with a hand on the blanket behind her. "Do you remember our family bonfires out here when we were kids?"

"I do. They were so fun. Dad and I talked about that not too long ago. I should send him a picture. Hold on." Mason dug around the bottom of the basket and found his cell phone. "Selfie!" He angled the camera so the bonfire was behind them. Linda smiled as she leaned closer to his shoulder.

Once he clicked the picture, Linda leaned in to look. "That's good. Send it to me, please."

"Same number?"

"Yeah." She'd never changed it, hoping he'd reach out.

"You got it." His thumbs tapped on his phone. "That's what I was going to say, too. I remember having bonfires when we were kids. My Mom would bake cookies and your mom would bring the salty snacks, chips or popcorn. It was great! Fun times."

"Your mom made the best oatmeal raisin cookies. I miss them. I miss her."

She heard Mason's breath hitch and worried she'd touched a nerve. "I'm sorry," she murmured.

"Please don't be." He turned towards her and held her gaze. "I don't get to talk about Mom enough. I miss her."

"She was the life of the party. She loved when we were all together."

"Being surrounded by people brought her joy. As soon as we left here, she'd be talking about the next time we could all come back."

He set his coffee down, wiggling it so the sand securely held it from under the blanket. He lay back and put his arms under his head as he searched the sky.

Linda turned to face the water. She watched the musician as he threw his head back to sing a long, lonesome note. She pulled her knees to her chest and rested her elbows on them, propping her head in her hands.

It was hard not to feel nostalgic and miss the days of their youth, before things got complicated with jobs, travel, and broken hearts.

The sun had set, and the horizon glowed with streaks of pink and purple. Linda thought the combination was gorgeous and considered adding purple streaks to her hair. A stab of irritation followed, thinking about her sister's demands to dye it dark blonde or brown for her wedding. Why did Laurel have to be so controlling all the time?

Mr. Cowboy Hat launched into a Kenny Chesney song about sunsets, and Linda felt a tear trickle down her face. She was thankful Mason was still lying on his back.

She brushed the moisture away and reached for her coffee cup.

Mason put his hand on her lower back, though he didn't move the rest of his body. "Hey, what's wrong?"

"How did you..." She turned to look at him. How did he know? "It's nothing. Just feeling sentimental, I guess. Maybe I'm tired. It was an early start. Tomorrow will be another early morning. Maybe I should head in."

"Hey." Mason sat up. "We've only been here twenty minutes. It's too early to go to bed. It was my fault for saying I miss Mom. I didn't mean to bring you down."

"No, it's not that."

Sure, reminiscing was a part of it, but it was more about being in a romantic atmosphere with Mason and not being involved with him. When they were dating in college, she had fantasized about vacationing with him here, alone, without their families, but they'd never gotten a chance to do it. Now here they were together, but not *together*.

Her mind got stuck on a loop of 'what could have been', 'what almost was', and 'why not?' It was exhausting.

Mason put his arm around her and pulled her close. It felt good to rest her head on his shoulder. "Well," he said. "Whatever it is, I hope it passes. This night is too perfect to be sad. We're surrounded by some of the best seventy- and eighty-year-olds we're lucky to know. The bonfire is roaring, and this guy is halfway decent."

"Hey, he's fantastic."

Mason chuckled. "I suppose. How about a warmup on the coffee?"

"Now, that would be divine."

Mason filled their mugs and put the thermos back in the laundry basket. "Need your sweatshirt? It's cooled off."

"I do. Thanks."

She pulled the hoodie on and let the warmth envelop her. She closed her eyes to listen intently to the waves against the shore, which made a soothing backdrop to Mr. Cowboy Hat's crooning.

If she didn't think too much about all the could haves and should haves when it came to Mason, it was easy to let go and enjoy herself.

Chapter 10

On Wednesday, they dressed up like the Blues Brothers. Linda laughed every time she looked at herself in the mirror. She'd braided her hair and pinned it to the top of her head so it wouldn't show under her black fedora.

She didn't know how to tie a tie, so she left it loose around her neck. She'd ask Mason for help once he came to get her.

In the kitchen, she grabbed a couple of granola bars and apples and tossed them in her tote bag. Glancing at her laptop, she chewed on her lower lip. Once they were back from selling festival tickets, she had to complete Grady's proposal and submit it. She could not miss the 3 p.m. deadline.

The knock at the door pulled her eyes away from the PC. She opened the door for Mason and smiled to see him already wearing the dark sunglasses.

"Ready, Jake?"

"Jake?" her voice ticked up a notch. "I thought you'd be Jake, and I'd be Elwood."

"Elwood is taller."

"But Jake is stockier."

"Fine. I'll be a tall Jake. Ready, Elwood?"

"Almost," she laughed, loving that he'd given in. "Can you tie my tie? I have no clue."

"Sure." He stepped closer.

Standing so close to Mason, Linda caught the fresh scents of vanilla and citrus. His hands moved to her chest, and she forgot to breathe.

His eyes squinted, concentrating, and she was desperate to talk about something—the silence was too intense.

"Did you make coffee?" she asked.

"Uh, huh," he muttered. "Backpack in hall."

"Oh."

Mason flipped one end of the tie over and it fluttered before her eyes. As he concentrated, she studied his face. His eyebrows twitched up and down as he worked on the tie. Once again, Linda's fingers itched to reach out and smooth his brow. She fought to keep them down.

Too soon, he stepped back and said, "Ta da! It's hard to do that on someone else. I can tie my own tie without thinking about it."

She glanced down. "Thanks. It looks good. Ready?"

This being her third day spending time with Mason, Linda felt herself relaxing a little more. She pushed the memories of dating Mason, both at sixteen and twenty-two, out of her mind. She hoped that by the end of their time together next week, they would have reformed their friendship. She'd be content with that.

It would be fun to call and text him again. Exchange funny stories about their lives. Maybe after this time together, they could even chat about future dating attempts, and it would not be weird. She still needed a date for her sister's wedding. It couldn't be Mason, though. That would be too awkward around their families.

That's why they'd broken up at sixteen. Their sisters' teasing was too much. Once Laurel and Erin knew they were dating, their relationship was ruined. Their sisters had teased them mercilessly. They'd decided it was easier to go back to being friends. Besides, they had lived an hour apart, gone to different schools, had different circles of friends—not ideal circumstances for a solid relationship at the vulnerable age of sixteen.

When they got back together in college, it felt different, and right. Their sisters no longer teased, they were both focused on school and "too mature" to tease. That was fine with Mason and Linda. Not having the family pressure made their relationship easier.

Driving to the grocery store, Linda asked Mason if he'd decided on his next nursing assignment.

He frowned as he slowed for a stop sign. "No decision yet," he said. "Why?"

Linda stared at the water bottle in her hand. "Just curious." She didn't want him to think she was *concerned.* "Don't you have to let them know before you show up? Is there a date you have to decide by?"

"Yes, next Tuesday. I have a call scheduled with the agency's placement manager. I'll have to decide by then. I may flip a coin." He shrugged.

Linda considered his offhand remark. She couldn't imagine flipping a coin to decide something as important as where a person was going to live. She'd never lived far from where she grew up. Moving two hours away within her home state seemed radical to her.

She turned to watch the scenery fly by and clasped her hands in her lap. She wasn't a consideration in where he'd live next. Not that she expected to be! They'd only reconnected four days ago. She wouldn't even consider them good friends again yet. He shouldn't consider her in decisions that affected his life. But a tiny part of her wished she could be a factor. If they lived closer together, maybe she could come to terms with their past, heal, and move on.

After their volunteer shift, forty-five tickets sold, and many selfies, Mason suggested stopping for lunch before going back to the condo. They ate lunch at a small roadside "Crab Shack" and Linda prayed the seafood was fresh, as the venue looked sketchy.

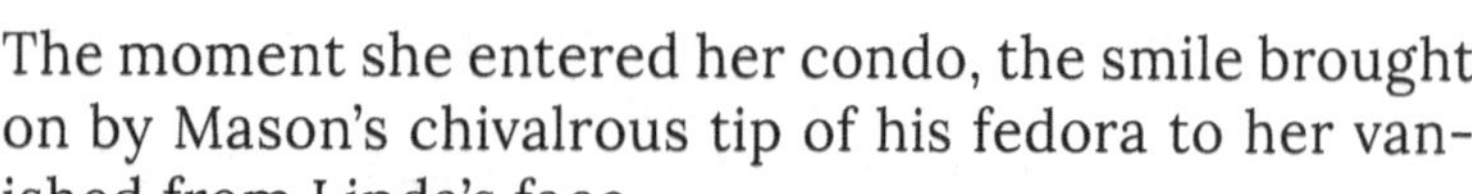

The moment she entered her condo, the smile brought on by Mason's chivalrous tip of his fedora to her vanished from Linda's face.

"Oh, no!" she muttered as she rushed over to her PC. While enjoying a leisurely lunch with Mason, she'd forgotten the deadline, and it was looming fast. Glancing at the digital time display on her phone, she cursed and dropped everything. Her tote bag flopped to the floor; her phone and keys dropped on the table.

She had fifteen minutes. She hit the power button on the laptop. "I can do this," she told herself. Her leg was bouncing up and down like a two-year-old after a bowl of ice cream.

"Come on, come on," she whined to the machine as the loading indicator flashed at her. She debated calling Grady. If she pulled this off, he wouldn't have to know. And there was no way he could swoop in and save the day now. All the information was on her computer.

"Ugh." She grabbed her cell phone and punched Grady's speed dial. She had to call him. There was too much at stake.

"Yes?" he answered, his "I'm at work" voice clear.

"Grady. I'm not sure I can make the three o'clock deadline. I was gone later than I planned and still need to put the numbers together. It's going to take me a little time."

"What can I do?"

"Say a prayer?"

He huffed. "Call me at 3:01."

"Yes." She hung up.

She looked at her notes. She hoped the last estimate was in her inbox. Mr. Peña had said he'd send it this morning. She should have called earlier to confirm he'd sent it or remind him of the urgency.

Her eyes scanned her inbox. Not there. She called Mr. Peña and picked up her pen, tapping it nervously on the notebook beside her.

"Al-lo," he answered. She always wondered why he said hello that way.

"Hey, Guillermo. I need that estimate. Now. I was expecting it this morning!" The desperation was clear in her voice.

"I sent you it."

She glanced at her inbox again. "No...I don't see an email from you. Do you have the total number for me? I can write it down." She wanted to cry. Only ten minutes remained.

"I sent it."

"I know. You said that. But I don't have it."

"I can't keep all the estimates in my brain."

She suppressed a groan. "We talked about this yesterday. You said you were in the four-thousand-dollar ballpark. Does that help?"

He clucked his tongue a few times. As stressed as she was, it still made her smile.

"Yes," he finally said. "Yes. Umm. I'm pretty sure the estimate landed around..." he paused again. "Six thousand, two hundred and fifty dollars."

She wrote the number down. "Wow, that didn't land in the ballpark."

"Knocked it out of the park."

"Yeah," she said, "that expression doesn't really work in this case. But that's okay. I needed the number. No time to debate your estimation accuracy. Thanks!"

She hung up and opened the spreadsheet with all the estimates for this project. She searched for Mr. Peña's company name. Finding it, she slid his number in place and scrolled to the bottom to get the total.

Gulping, she was glad this wasn't her tentative project with the large financial risk. She preferred her financial risk to be in the one to twenty-dollar range. Grady's risk came with at least four zeros after the ten. At least.

She opened the PowerPoint presentation and jumped to page eight, entering the grand total.

Glancing at the clock, she audibly swallowed. It was already three minutes after the hour. She was late. Tears popped in her eyes.

"No. No," she lamented. She was even late calling Grady back.

Concentrating, she opened the email in her drafts folder, entered the grand total within the email, and attached the PowerPoint presentation. Maybe, just maybe, there would be a reprieve if she sent it in five minutes late.

After clicking a few more buttons, she hit send and leaned back in her chair. She blew out a long breath. She dreaded calling Grady back, but she knew bad news didn't age well. Better to get it over with. She dialed his number.

"Well?" he asked.

"I submitted it five minutes late. Hopefully, they'll accept and review it." Was it wishful thinking?

Grady was quiet.

"I know I screwed this up, Grady. I'm so sorry. It's not like me to miss things like this. I had a busy morning and went to lunch, and the deadline slipped my mind. I should have been back in time to make sure I had the full estimate, so I wouldn't be late."

Grady sighed. "I'm disappointed, to say the least. You said you would work while in Florida, that nothing would fall through the cracks. This could be a canyon-sized crack."

"I know." The acid in her stomach bubbled.

"We'll see what happens. But it was a hard deadline."

"I know."

She hated repeating herself, and her head pounded.

Grady said a terse goodbye and hung up. Linda sat and brushed hot tears from her cheeks.

This day had started out wonderfully. She felt she was coming to a new place of contentment with Mason. The bitter memories of the Mason who'd broken her heart were being replaced by present-day Mason, who was funny and kind.

She could see the traits that made him an exceptional nurse. This morning, while they were selling tickets, Mason had helped six women and four men (yes, she'd counted) push their carts and load their groceries. That was Mason. He would not sit still if someone needed him.

Taking a deep breath, she shut down her laptop and glanced outside. The sun danced across the water, and reflections of light mirrored the movement on the ceiling. She dashed to the bedroom to change out of the dark suit, pulling on a bikini covered by a pair of white shorts and a yellow tank top. She'd sit on the balcony and catch some rays while she chastised herself for her mistake.

She poured a large glass of peach margarita. No, the alcohol wouldn't solve her problems, but it might help her forget them for a while.

Stepping onto the balcony, she tossed a beach towel on a chair and placed her beverage and book on the small table next to it.

"Oh, hey," Mason called from his balcony.

"Shoot!" She tipped forward, tripping on her flip-flop. She glanced over at Mason. He stood with humongous dumbbells, doing curls or lifts or...why was he wearing a tank top? His exposed biceps could cause a traffic accident. "Couldn't make it to a gym?"

"Got everything I need here. Saves driving and waiting. Besides, it helps when I wake up at three in the morning and can't sleep. I can jump out of bed, lift some iron, and eventually I go back to sleep."

"Oh." She sat in her chair and picked up the book. "What do you do when you're not here? You certainly don't lug those things around the country with you."

He smiled, set the weights down and picked up a glass of water. After taking a long drink, he responded. "I try to find apartments with twenty-four-hour gyms."

"Logical." Watching him workout made her thirsty. She took a large sip of the margarita, dropped her head back, and sighed.

"Are you all right?" Mason had walked to the edge of his balcony and was only a few feet away.

"No."

"Want to talk about it?"

"No."

"I'm climbing over."

"No!" Linda leaned forward and turned towards him. He was lifting a leg. "You can't do that. What if you fell? My unbelievably horrible day could get that much worse!"

"Bad day? You were with me all day. I'm coming over. Let me in the front door if you don't want me climbing over."

She rolled her eyes and shook her head, but stood up and walked through her condo. Mason was at the door before she opened it.

"Did you run?" she asked.

He twisted his lips comically. "Maybe?"

She motioned him inside and he followed her back to the balcony.

Mason sat in the open seat and picked up her glass. He took a big whiff and said, "Whew. That's strong. What's going on, Lindy?"

She plopped down on her chair. "I messed up a work assignment. Turned it in late, and it may have cost my boss a huge opportunity." She felt tears welling up again. She did not want to cry in front of Mason. Dropping her sunglasses back down onto her nose, she was thankful she had still been wearing the dark Wayfarers.

Mason pretended to look at a watch on his wrist. "Umm, we've been apart for forty-seven minutes. How could you have possibly screwed up in that amount of time?"

"Believe me, I can get in trouble in forty-seven seconds." She let out an exasperated breath. "Had a hard three o'clock deadline. Missed it by five minutes. I feel like a complete idiot. My boss is mad. This could cost him thousands of dollars. It's a horrible mistake."

"It's not life or death, though." He leaned towards her, and his voice was soft. He'd probably seen life and death mistakes.

She huffed out a breath. "I know it's not. For that, I'm extremely grateful. But I hate screwing up. It reminds me of all the ways I'm flawed. From my 'stupid hair colors,'" her fingers made air quotes, "to my 'can't get a date', to my 'too scared to leave home', to..." She stopped. Why was she blabbing like this to Mason? She glanced at her glass. It was almost empty. She'd pounded that drink. Not good.

"Hey." Mason reached over and clasped her hand. "Take a deep breath." He paused and took a deep breath, holding it in until she followed suit. When she did, he let his breath out slowly, encouraging her to do the same. "There. Mistakes happen. Live, learn, move on. Don't beat yourself up over them. You'll drive yourself bonkers. I know what you need. You need a movie night. If I remember correctly, old musicals were your thing. Are they still?"

Linda smiled. She adored old musicals. "Yes. How can you be upset when you're watching *Singing in the Rain* or *Guys and Dolls*?"

Mason nodded. "That's what I thought. Well, six-thirty. My place. I'll bring the popcorn. You bring whatever you want—"

"A charcuterie board!"

"Excuse you?"

"Do you ever get a chance to hang out with human beings, or do you work *all* the time?"

"Work."

"Figures. A snack board. My specialty."

He smiled. "Sounds perfect. Should I make dinner? I'm an adequate chef when it comes to spaghetti and meatballs."

"Only if we can watch a movie while we eat."

"Indeed."

"I'll be there."

He left, and she closed her eyes, leaning back against the thick seat cushion. Taking a deep breath, she willed her body to relax. Mason's words had calmed her mind. She just needed her nerves to follow suit.

Chapter 11

Mason glanced around the kitchen. Slightly messy, but not destroyed. A plus. Linda would be over any minute now. He glanced at his smartwatch and saw the seconds tick toward six thirty. He started a silent countdown as he motioned his finger at the door on the beat. Four, three, two....

As his watch ticked on the half hour, there was a knock on the door. He'd suspected she'd be that punctual.

Throwing the door open, he grinned at her and swept his arm back. "Welcome! Come in!"

Lindy had on a pink Minnie Mouse T-shirt, black yoga pants, and socks. No shoes. It looked like she'd recently showered, as her hair was damp.

Like taking someone's pulse, he was hyperaware of each second ticking by. Her casual appearance was comforting, made him think about that magical place called "home". There wouldn't need to be countless dates getting to know her. He knew her. Knew her choice in movies, knew the foods she liked to eat, knew she rooted for the underdog, knew she was fiercely independent.

But though he knew all those things about her, his knowledge was old. How had the last six years changed her? There was a lot to catch up on. He hoped, before they each left here, they'd have made progress in rekindling their friendship.

Even thinking this, he knew he'd have to work hard to make her see that he had grown, knew he'd hurt her when he'd left, and would prove himself worthy of her time, attention, and perhaps affection.

Jolting him out of his romantic thoughts, she breezed by him with a large tray filled with little mounds of food, tightly wrapped with clear plastic wrap.

"Wow," he said. "You know I made dinner, right?"

Linda laughed as she set the tray on the counter in the kitchen. He'd followed closely behind her and leaned over her shoulder to look at the assortment of goodies. There were pretzels, crackers, three kinds of olives, several varieties of nuts, neatly arranged rows of cheeses, something that looked like jam, and bunches of green and red grapes.

"That is a work of art," he said, with a low whistle.

"Thank you. I ran to the store to pick up some extra munchies." Linda turned and smiled at him. He could smell the lilac fragrance of her soap or light perfume. He pictured her sitting on a blanket in a field of flowers and smiled.

She was so close; he could lean down and kiss her. *Whoa!* He was trying to cheer her up, not cause her to run out of the condo like it was on fire.

"Hungry?" He moved around her to the stove and stirred the pasta sauce.

"Smells wonderful in here. Have to say I was worried. I remember your frequent ramen noodle dinners in college."

"Dinner, lunch, and breakfast. I've learned a few things since then. Here, plate up. I have everything else we need on the coffee table. The movie will commence in five minutes."

"And? What movie are we starting with?"

"Luckily for you, Dad doesn't believe in getting rid of anything, and I found boxes of DVDs in the closet. We've got *Guys and Dolls*, *The Sound of Music*, and *My Fair Lady*. You get to pick. They're all in the living room."

"*Guys and Dolls*, please!"

"You're on."

They fixed their plates and took them to the living area. Mason suggested eating on the coffee table to prevent spaghetti sauce stains on the couch.

"Not a problem." Linda put down her plate and glanced around. "I'm still surprised that this place has stayed the same all these years. I adore the sea turtles in that painting. It makes me happy."

"Remember what I said about dad not throwing anything out?" Mason asked, his eyes scanning the room. "Case in point. He says there is no need to change anything when it still looks great."

They sat on the floor at the coffee table, like they had as kids. Mason had a basket of garlic bread and a bottle of red wine on the coffee table. He poured each of them a glass and offered the bread to Linda. She took a piece, was quiet for a minute, then said, "You think he keeps it the same to remember your mom?"

"Wow. I thought he was just a tightwad. Maybe you're right."

Mason pondered the idea. Maybe she *was* right. Maybe it was a way for his dad to keep the memory of his mom alive. Subtle. He thought back to last Christmas when his stepmom Terry was pleading for the chance to make over the condo, but Christopher held his ground and refused. Mason had thought his dad was being an ogre, but maybe there'd been something more to it. He'd have to give that some more consideration.

"So, any update on the work snafu?"

Linda swirled noodles on her fork. "No, we might not hear anything for a day or two. I hope the seller considers Grady's offer."

"What's your boss like? A tyrant?"

Mason loved asking the questions. He got more time to eat while she considered and answered.

"No," Linda protested. "Grady's wonderful." She took a sip of wine, and Mason's muscles went rigid. He told himself to chill. Linda hadn't acted like she *liked* her boss, but the sound of his name caused heartburn, anyway. Or maybe that was the garlic in the spaghetti sauce.

"He's smart, clear with direction, open." Her eyes lit up. "I love working for him. I have a great setup, working from home; he allows me to have a flexible schedule. I don't have to get dressed..."

She paused at the worst possible time. Now Mason was thinking about her "not dressed". He groaned.

"What's wrong?" Her head twisted quickly, glancing down. "Did you spill something?"

"Uh, no. I remembered I was going to bake a cake. Forgot."

She gave him the funniest, sweetest, quizzical look. She didn't buy it, and she seemed to consider calling him out on it. He could tell. He'd seen that look many times.

"You were saying about Grady..." Mason didn't like the taste of the guy's name on his tongue.

"Right." She looked back at her plate and picked up a piece of garlic bread. He knew she preferred the garlic bread to the spaghetti; she always had. "Grady. He's great. I love working for him."

"Have you ever dated him?"

"What? No. Why would you ask that?"

He studied his fork carefully. "Don't know. You seemed gushy about him."

"Gushy? Is that a legit word? You're hilarious. No, never had feelings for him. And he's in a great relationship with an amazing lady. I love her."

"That's good." He paused and looked at her. "I apologize for making you late. I shouldn't have suggested we stop for lunch."

"Mason, it's not your fault. It's all mine. I should have paid closer attention to the time."

"Well, I hope, whatever happens, that it works out in the end. Please don't beat yourself up over it. Life's too short. Ready to start the movie? Marlon's waiting."

He needed to stop grilling her about her boss. His heart was racing, like he was walking through a haunted house, wanting to know what was around the next corner, but not wanting to know.

She said she didn't have feelings for her boss. Good. There must not be a significant other in her life, as the dating list on her refrigerator that she wouldn't let him see suggested. Sorcha wouldn't have made her write out a list of things to look for in a guy if there was someone. *That's even better.*

Maybe he should ask to be her date for Laurel's wedding. There was no question he was going; it was a given. And if Linda needed a date...but would she think it was a good idea?

He'd give it a few more days before broaching the subject. He needed more time to smooth the rough edges and broken pieces of their friendship. Then he could get a read on whether there could be more.

Thirty minutes into the movie, Linda hit the pause button on the remote. "Quick break? Gotta pee."

"Sure. I'll pick up dinner plates and bring the charter board over."

"Charcuterie board."

"Bless you."

She stood and arched her back. "Ha. Ha. I'm moving to the couch. Can't sit on the floor for hours like I did when I was eight."

"Same."

When the movie ended, Linda said she needed to go to bed, and Mason wanted to pull her back onto the couch when she stood. He'd hoped she would stay for a second movie. As the evening went on, he saw the stress lift from her shoulders. She even got up and danced during the "Luck Be a Lady" number.

After she left, he sat on the couch facing the place where she'd been. The throw pillow she'd hugged most of the night was lying down and he reached for it to stand it up in its proper position. Instead, he pulled it to his chest and bent his head over it. It held her sweet floral scent. He inhaled deeply and took the pillow to bed with him.

Closing the door behind her, Linda leaned against it and took a deep breath. She hadn't been sure what to expect tonight, but it still surprised her. Spending time with Mason reminded her of everything she'd ever loved about him. This time with him was overriding the painful memories of their breakup.

Pushing off the door and entering the clean kitchen, she set the nearly empty charcuterie board on the counter. She put the few remaining items away and rinsed off the board. Pouring a glass of water from the filter dispenser, she grabbed her phone to text Sorcha.

Linda: You still up?

Sorcha: Yes, but I'm out. Met up with coworkers for drinks.

Linda: Oh. Nice. Can we talk tomorrow?

It was probably best that Sorcha couldn't talk tonight. Linda needed to reassess her feelings about Mason before laying out her thoughts to her roommate.

Sorcha: What's wrong?

How did she know? Linda smiled. This is what best friends were for.

Linda: Not important. Enjoy your evening. Call me tomorrow afternoon.

Looking at her laptop, she groaned. Spending the evening with Mason, she had forgotten about her work screw-up. She wished she'd put the laptop and all work-related items away before she'd gone to Mason's condo. Then maybe she could have come back and gone to bed without the worry and stress that now threatened to keep her awake all night.

She hurried past the table. She'd wash her face, crawl into bed, and read until she fell asleep. Maybe then her work error wouldn't cause bad dreams.

Chapter 12

Linda checked her email inbox before leaving Thursday morning. No word from the sellers about Grady's proposal. They didn't acknowledge that they had it or that it was submitted too late. She tried to stay positive; sometimes no news was good news.

She was waiting in the hallway for Mason when he walked out of his family's condo. She knew he'd be on time, so she didn't bother knocking.

When he stepped out, he smiled as his eyes met hers.

"No knocking? Just stalking?" he asked, following her to the elevator.

"Not stalking, just waiting. I knew you'd be on time." She swung her tote bag as she pressed the elevator button.

Mason was wearing the outfit they'd found while thrifting—purple bell-bottom corduroy pants, a plain white T-shirt, and a pink floral vest with a matching scarf that he had tied around his head. He had a pair of John Lennon-style glasses with purple lenses.

They'd ditched the idea of being Parrot-heads when Mason found the corduroy pants.

Linda glanced down at her own clothes. She'd found a pink floral dress, a peace symbol pendant on a long, black cord, and a pair of round pink sunglasses. She was thankful for the long, loose dress. It was already eighty degrees outside, and it wasn't even seven o'clock.

"You're going to roast in those pants," she said to Mason as they stepped onto the elevator.

"I'm hoping for a strong breeze." He held up a small cooler. "I have extra bottles of water and cooling cloths. Wouldn't want to faint in the heat when I look this groovy!"

Linda laughed and rolled her eyes.

The morning flew by. Since there was a steady stream of shoppers in and out of the grocery store and it was the last day before the festival began, Linda and Mason sold tickets steadily.

When their time was up, Linda glanced into the money box and gasped. "Wow," she said. "Meri is going to flip when she sees how many tickets we sold."

Mason nodded. "We couldn't sell them fast enough! Can't wait to tell her."

He opened the cooler, pulled out a cooling towel, and poured water over it. He shook it gently to activate the cooling fibers and placed it around his neck. "I'm not getting into the car in these hot pants. Wait here. I'm going inside to change."

He dashed into the grocery store, and Linda gathered their items, folded up the store's chairs, and set them and the table against the wall. The manager would send someone out to take them back inside.

When Mason returned he was wearing shorts and a fresh gray T-shirt.

"Better?" she asked.

"Much." He nodded.

"Wish I'd thought to bring a change of clothes."

"I should have suggested it before we left." As they made their way towards the car, Mason asked if Linda had afternoon plans.

"I need to process Grady's accounts payable today, but that won't take more than an hour. And I can do it anytime."

Mason clicked the remote to unlock the trunk and tossed in the cooler and his bag. Linda added her extra stuff as well.

"Hey, any news on the proposal you submitted yesterday?" he asked.

Linda was thankful he didn't add "late" to his question. "No. Not yet. I'm trying not to worry about it. It's out of my hands now. I can only accept responsibility, which I did, and wait."

"That's a healthy way of looking at it. I'm proud of you. Few people could do that so quickly." He unlocked the car. "Stand there with the door open for a minute. Let some of the heat out." He leaned in and started it.

"Does that actually work?"

"I think so. I'm too hot to get into a car that's a hundred and forty degrees. It's too hot to put the top down. We need the air-conditioning."

Linda nodded. "I wish they'd put awnings up over parking lots. Maybe even metal ones with solar panels on top. Win win."

"That would be cool. I saw that in a few places when I worked in Phoenix. I did a rotation there in July and August. The heat was brutal. I asked for third-shift rotations so I could sleep during the hottest part of the day."

"Wow. That makes sense, but I imagine a third shift would be hard to adjust in and out of. Hard to manage a dating life."

Linda regretted the words as soon as they were out of her mouth. They had talked about dating before, and Mason said he didn't date often. Now, by bringing it up again, it sounded like she cared. She didn't. Did she?

Mason motioned for her to get in and he sat in the driver's seat. He fiddled with the air-conditioning and shut his door. For a moment, Linda thought he would not respond to her statement.

"There was zero dating life in Phoenix. It was too hot." Mason turned and smiled at her as he put the car in reverse to pull out of the parking space. He then deftly changed the subject. "So, you have an hour of work. What do you say to grabbing a sandwich at Crabbie's and then heading to the pool? It's too hot to do much else."

"That sounds great. Stopping at Crabbie's on the way, or going back to the condo and then to Crabbie's?" She wanted to change out of this dress.

"Condo. You want to change, don't you?"

"Desperately."

"Fine." He paused as he pulled up to a stop sign, checking both directions. "But I think you are the cutest flower child. I'd be proud to walk in there with you. Heck, I might have to fight some guy off you again."

Linda laughed. "No guy would hit on me in this granny dress." She picked up the skirts of the dress and shook it.

"I wouldn't be so sure of that. You're a beauty no matter what you're wearing. That dress doesn't hide your beautiful face and radiant smile."

"Um, what's with the flattery, Mason? Are you trying to butter me up for something? Need a kidney? My firstborn?"

Mason chuckled. "I don't need anything. I'm serious."

"That laugh disproves your point."

"Ha! Wait. Do you want to get your work done before we go to lunch? I'm hungry, but I could wait."

Linda considered. "I would like to get it done before lunch. Feeling like I'm already in hot water with my boss. I don't want him to think I'm completely slacking while I'm here. But if you're hungry, give me a few minutes and I'll throw together a few snacks to hold us over."

"Another chartery-board."

"Charcuterie board. But no. Just cheese and crackers. Or I could put together a lunch spread, and we wouldn't need to go to Crabbie's. It would be better on my bank account, anyway. And I already bought the groceries."

"That's fine. I can contribute cold cuts and a loaf of sourdough bread I picked up yesterday afternoon. I make a mean turkey-and-ham sandwich."

Linda smiled. "I remember. You were the king of sandwiches in college."

"I'm still the king. And now I can afford deli bread."

"Nice."

It was nice. Easy. They were falling into a comfortable place again. Linda just needed to remind herself that this was temporary. This serendipitous meet-up with Mason was allowing her heart to heal. She was confident that by the time they left, they'd be on friendly terms. She could live with that.

Back at the condo building, Mason parked, and they went to Meri's office to give her the money box and remaining tickets.

When they showed her the number of tickets sold, she let out a squeal. "Why, the Almighty knew I needed some good news today. And mercy, Lindy, look at that dress. Is it polyester? Aren't you hot?"

"Yes, it is." Linda nodded. "And I'm roasting."

"But isn't she adorable, Meri?" Mason asked.

Meri cut her eyes to Mason quickly. Mason braced himself for Meri's response. Maybe he shouldn't have said that.

"Why, yes, she is. As always," Meri said slowly. "I hope you didn't go like that," she looked Mason up and down. "You look like you're going out for beers with the boys, and she looks like a hippy."

"Flower child." Linda said.

"Same thing," Meri said.

"Really? Wow," Linda responded. "Well, I am going to change. Good luck with the festival, Meri."

"Wait a second." Meri held up her hand. "As a thank-you to you both for helping this week, I want to give you festival tickets. I assume you didn't buy any yourself."

"We didn't," Mason said. "Thank you! That's wonderful. Wasn't expecting that. Should be a great time."

Meri handed each of them a ticket and shooed them out of her office.

In the elevator, Linda asked for twenty minutes to take a cool shower and change before Mason came for lunch.

"Not a problem. I'll change into my swim trunks and pack necessities for the pool, so we can go as soon as you're done with work."

Entering the condo, Linda tossed her bag on the counter and grabbed a Coke from the fridge. She leaned against the counter and popped the can open. She took a long gulp of the soft drink and burped; thankful she was alone. A starfish magnet on the fridge was upside down, so she straightened it. It must have gotten flipped when she pulled the "Wedding Date" criteria list off before Mason could see it.

She'd felt annoyed at Sorcha when she suggested the list. But to her credit, the idea came about after Linda had spent a long time, too long, ranting about how she would never find a guy to date, let alone fall in love with. She'd claimed that her list of must-haves was a mile long, and no guy would meet all the requirements on her list.

Sorcha had called foul and suggested they write out the list. As she'd suspected, the list wasn't all that long; Linda had gotten too hung up on the fact that she hadn't made it to a fourth date in over three years, counting her losses before giving dates a chance to succeed.

Sorcha thought Wyatt, the new guy at their favorite local coffee shop, had a thing for Linda and that he'd ask Linda out if she'd show him the tiniest bit of interest.

Linda stated that Wyatt's extreme handsomeness intimidated her too much, and she wouldn't contemplate going out with him even if there was a glitch in the matrix and he felt attracted to her.

Maybe Sorcha was right, and Linda checked out of dating before giving the guy a chance. But breaking things off after a couple of dates was easier than falling for someone and then getting your heart broken. Every breakup left her hollow and crushed, like a cicada shell a child had pulled off a tree and stomped on.

Sorcha's advice was sinking in. Linda had hoped that getting away from home, spending some fun time with Sorcha and then some alone time, would give her the kick in the butt to try dating again.

She hoped that by the time this working vacation was over and she returned home, that she'd have summoned up the nerve to ask Wyatt out for something other than coffee.

If they got along well and made it past a date or two, Wyatt might even be a great date for Laurel's wedding. He had movie-star good looks and rock-star charm.

But if things didn't work out with Wyatt, she'd still need a date to Laurel's wedding. There was no way she was going alone.

Setting the soda on the counter, she walked to the garbage can and fished out the criteria list to see how Wyatt might measure up. He obviously met the 'attractive or cute' requirement. He was 'kind' and 'funny', to her, and any other guest she'd seen him interact with. She sensed he might be 'spontaneous', 'fun', and 'creative', but she wasn't a hundred percent sure. There was no way to know if he liked 'cats' or 'musicals'. She suspected he liked 'live music' as he frequently wore T-shirts featuring eighties and nineties rock bands, like Nirvana, Pearl Jam, Soundgarden, and Foo Fighters.

Tossing the list back into the garbage, Linda grabbed her soda can and walked to the bathroom. She mused over the fact that the list wasn't very long. She needed to get back out there and try dating again. Get back on the horse. She could do this. She needed a shower, some time to journal, to forgive Mason, and to move on.

Chapter 13

When Mason knocked on her door, Linda called out for him to let himself in. She was in the bathroom, braiding her hair into two high braids, which she would twist into buns on top of her head. She knew there was a sun visor that would keep the sun off her face and accommodate the hair style. A regular ball cap or straw hat would not.

"Where are you?" Mason called, entering the condo.

"Bathroom." Linda stepped into the hallway and waved at him. "I'll be right out."

"All right. I'll set up sandwich fixings on the counter. I assumed you had condiments, so I didn't bring any. Good assumption?"

"Good assumption."

"Perfection."

Linda twisted the second braid and secured the bun with two pins. She slicked on some pink lip balm with SPF. She shoved it into a pocket, realizing she'd need it again after she ate.

Mason was cutting thick slices of bread when she emerged from the bathroom. While her Aunt Sandy liked to change the decor in the condo often, nothing changed in where she kept kitchen essentials. Mason made himself at home, grabbing a cutting board, a knife, and a plate to lay the bread slices on.

"Hey, hey!" he said, glancing up at her. "Cute hairstyle. You look like you're ready for the pool."

"Not quite. I still need to go through emails and follow up on a couple of items for work. You don't mind if I do that while you fix your sandwich, do you?"

"Course not."

"There's a plate of cheese and fruit in the fridge. Pull it out if you want some."

"Sure. Don't mind me. Get your work done so we can go play."

Linda smiled. He'd said those words to her countless times growing up. He brought the snack plate to the table, and she nibbled as she worked. When his sandwich was ready, he grabbed a soda and brought his lunch to the table.

"Are you okay if I eat here?" he asked, sitting across from her.

"Yeah. It's fine."

She picked up a few grapes and chewed them slowly. Her eyes started wandering over to Mason's sandwich.

"Wow. That looks amazing." The bread slices were thick, and he'd piled several layers of lettuce leaves and tomatoes among the sliced turkey and cheese.

"I must say, it is." He nodded, his eyes flashing with humor and something else Linda couldn't place. "Want me to make you one?"

"No, thanks. Working." She turned her eyes back to the laptop, but the image of Mason's eyes continued to flit across her mind.

She hit send on an email and marked an item off her list.

Scrunching her nose, she tried to remember the color of Wyatt's eyes. She thought they were blue, but she wasn't certain. Mason's brown eyes always reminded her of her favorite fuzzy blanket. They were warm and cozy and made you feel good when you looked at them.

She completed her necessary work as Mason finished his sandwich. Closing her laptop, she said, "I think I'll make a sandwich and take it down to the pool with me.

I'm not ready to eat right now. And I'm ready for some pool time."

"Yes!" Mason pumped his fist in the air. "Let's pack a cooler. Is there still one in the front closet?"

"Yes. Right where it belongs."

She'd put it back when she and Sorcha returned from the beach. The other benefit of staying at a family-owned condo instead of a hotel was that, apart from food, most anything they needed for vacation was in the unit. The front closet was packed with life jackets, snorkels, beach towels, tote bags, coolers, extra flip-flops (mostly for guests who'd forgotten to bring them), sand toys, blow-up floats, boogie boards, a portable horseshoe game set, and "sand-proof" beach blankets. Her aunt and uncle were considerate of their guests' needs. A condo on the beach drew lots of friends and family, sometimes on short notice.

Mason grabbed the cooler, dumped the ice from the freezer in, and peeked in the refrigerator for beverages. "What are you in the mood for?"

"Grab a couple cans of Coke and a couple of seltzers. I'll grab bottles for water."

Her Aunt Sandy was anti-bottled water. She'd had an upscale water-filtration system put into the unit and bought many stainless steel water bottles. She said she preferred the taste of the water she filled herself. And she was anti-plastic and pro recycling.

Linda, too, was mindful of environmental effects and was happy to bottle her own water. She didn't have the fancy water-filtration system at home, but her filtration pitcher worked just fine.

Soon they had everything they needed and started for the door.

"Oh, wait. I forgot my book." Linda rushed to the bedroom and grabbed the book she was reading off the nightstand. She dropped into her tote, and out the door they went.

Mason worried he was babbling away like a three-year-old as they made their way down the elevator and out to the pool.

At this time of the day, the building was blocking the sun from one side of the pool, and several residents were happily sitting or lounging in the shade.

Mason raised an eyebrow at Linda as they passed through the blue safety fence surrounding the large kidney-bean-shaped pool.

Linda gestured towards two loungers that were still in the sun, and Mason proceeded to that corner. He was pleased that she pointed away from the other guests. He wanted alone time with Linda, not to share her companionship with Mr. Green or the others.

As they settled into their corner, putting beach towels on the lounge chairs, Mr. Green walked over to say hello. He chatted briefly, saying it was too hot in the sun to chitchat, and returned to his shady side of the pool.

Linda grabbed a bottle of sunscreen out of her tote and tossed it to Mason. "Will you put some lotion on my back?" she asked.

I thought you'd never ask. "Sure, if you'll return the favor."

Linda laughed softly. "I think our parents would be proud of the responsible adults we've become."

"Indeed! I thought my mom's head would explode when she reminded us for the one millionth time to use sunblock. It was a recurring sound of summer. If my mom wasn't reminding us, your mom was."

Mason moved his hands slowly, methodically, over Linda's back and shoulders, enjoying the feel of her silky-smooth skin. If she questioned him, he could say he was making sure she had enough lotion. He wouldn't drag it out so long it got weird. Probably.

"Certainly," Linda said, dropping her head forward as he touched the back of her neck. "Well, they drilled it into us."

Once Mason had thoroughly covered Linda's back (twice), he handed the bottle back and sat on her chair with his back to her. From his vantage point, he was looking directly at the five senior residents on the other side of the pool. He waved and hoped they would stay in place.

He had to suppress a groan as Linda applied lotion to the back of his arms. He contemplated jumping in the pool immediately and then asking for more lotion as a "safety precaution".

Lotion applied, Mason reluctantly moved back to his lounge chair and pulled a small portable speaker out of his bag, connecting it to his phone so they could listen to music. He found a playlist of his favorite summer music and pushed play. "Walking on Sunshine" by Katrina and the Waves started playing, and he leaned back and put his sunglasses on.

"You're ridiculous," Linda said.

"How do you figure?"

"First of all, those sunglasses are hideous, and second of all, this is your summer playlist, and the first song hasn't changed in over six years."

"Sunglasses came from the basket in the condo. I didn't want to wear my expensive ones out here. I take care of my stuff. And I'll happily replace this pair of ten-dollar rando glasses if I lose them. I've added songs to the list, but this is still my favorite summer song. So, make fun of me all you want."

He didn't mind the teasing at all. It felt like Linda was letting her guard down around him. She seemed freer than she had five days ago when they'd first reconnected.

Has it only been five days? The hollowness of the years without her was fading. It was feeling more and more like it'd been a few months since he'd seen her last, not six long and soulless years.

They still had a long way to go to get back to where they'd been before he'd lost his mind and run, but he was hopeful they were on the right path.

He watched Linda pull stuff out of her bag and get situated. Her large bottle of water with the "Seaside Bay" logo went on the concrete next to her right hand. The small handheld, battery-operated fan that squirted water to keep you cool went next to the water bottle. Two magazines and a book entitled "Buried in Bougainvillea: A Hibiscus Island Mystery" were on the beach towel next to her hand. Next, she pulled out a reusable silicone bag filled with pretzels, which she began eating.

She seemed to settle in, and Mason turned his gaze past her. From this vantage point, he could see a stretch of the white sand beach. There was a good assortment of tourists and locals having fun or lounging on the beach. He noticed a canopy being erected in front of the condo building next door.

"Look," he said. "Something's happening next door."

Linda glanced to where he pointed. "Hmm. Maybe Meri will know what's going on."

"Good call. I'll run and ask."

He enjoyed having a task to do. Even though he was supposed to be spending his time here in Florida chilling and making important decisions about what to do in life, he was best on his feet, moving and doing. That's why nursing was such a great role for him. He liked the fast pace, the constant interaction with patients, doctors, other nurses, office and technical staff. He loved meeting new people, which made the traveling gigs so appealing to him. But now, the thought of putting down roots again and making genuine, deep connections was taking on a new appeal.

He found Meri in her office, stirring a cup of tea and eyeing a plate of chocolate chip cookies.

"Hey, Meri! How's it going?"

"Ah, Mason." She lifted the plate of cookies, and offered them to him, but he declined. "I'll be better once we get through the festival this weekend. My phone has been ringing off the hook with last-minute emergencies. How can I help you?"

"Do you know what's going on next door? They're setting up a large canopy and moving tables onto the sand."

"Yes. They're having a luau tonight. Pig on a spit. Live music. And they'll have fireworks after dark. It's their building's fiftieth anniversary."

"Oh, cool. Think they'd mind a couple of interlopers?"

"Interlope away, young Mason." Her phone rang, and she shooed him away with her hand and a wink.

Mason whistled as he strolled through the rec room back to the pool. Now he had another mission to accomplish. Take Linda outside tonight to watch fireworks.

Chapter 14

Linda had her journal out when Mason returned from Meri's office. She was putting together a list of things she needed to do for Laurel's bridal shower, which was only four weeks away.

The planning activity allowed her to forget about missing the work deadline yesterday. Planning was her happy place. She felt in control and in her element when she was brainstorming and creating lists. Thinking about future accomplishments was better than focusing on past failures.

She already had the venue booked, and invitations were in the mail. She'd designed them and created a template to sell on her Etsy storefront.

"Whatcha doing?" Mason said as he approached.

"Working on plans for Laurel's bridal shower." She put the pen in the holder attached to the bright purple journal. "I need to call your sister to plan food and activities. We're co-hosting the shower. You know Laurel wouldn't trust me to do it all on my own."

"That sounds like Laurel. Anything I can do to help you?"

"No. I got it. Besides, what do you know about bridal showers?" Linda smiled at him as she adjusted the visor. It was too loose and kept slipping down onto her pink plastic sunglasses.

"To avoid them at all costs," Mason quipped. "Erin told me I got a wedding invitation at Dad's house. I need to RSVP."

"You do. Laurel will be happy to see you there." Linda looked away.

Would it be awkward with Mason there? Birds, not butterflies, seemed to fly around her chest, bumping against her ribcage.

She took a quick, deep breath and told herself to calm down. She desperately needed to find a date for Laurel's wedding if Mason was going to be there. Wondering if Mason would go solo or if he'd bring a date, she wasn't sure if she wanted to know the answer.

Mason lay back on the lounge and sighed. "Will you?"

"What?"

"Will you be happy to see me there?"

Linda took another deep breath; this could get painful in a hurry. There didn't seem to be a right answer to his question. Finally, she said, "Sure. It's an important event in our lives. I've always imagined our families together for the big moments, like weddings."

Mason made a noise in his throat, but Linda couldn't discern the meaning. To be safe, she decided not to ask.

Mason was quiet for so long that Linda thought he'd fallen asleep. She opened her journal again and stared at the list of qualities in a guy to date, which she'd jotted in her journal—easier to carry than the large piece of paper Sorcha had used. On a physical level, Wyatt matched her criteria nicely. She needed to get to know him better to see if his personality was a match.

"Who are you going with?" Mason asked.

She hadn't noticed that he'd sat up and was hovering close to her shoulder. She snapped her journal closed and hoped he hadn't seen the list.

"Don't know yet."

"So, you're not dating anyone seriously?"

Not dating anyone at all. To Mason she said, "Not really."

"Want to go with me?" he asked.

She sucked in a breath so loudly she imagined Meri could hear it inside the building. "What the what?" she sputtered.

"Be my date to Laurel's wedding."

Linda turned to look at him better and lowered her sunglasses, like she was trying to figure out what she was looking at. Mason smiled at her, and her heart fluttered.

"I don't think that will work," she said.

"Why not?"

"It would be too awkward. People will talk. It will take attention away from the bride, and people will vilify me for years to come. I'm supposed to be the boring, helpful, dull maid of honor. The bride is supposed to shine with the light of a thousand suns. They will shred me and toss me out with the trash if I take any attention away from Laurel. Not a good idea."

"Come on...you're full of unverified hypotheses. Take it down a notch."

Instead of irritating her, Mason's words made her smile. It was like Mason to be the voice of reason.

"Fine. Maybe I'm exaggerating a teeny, tiny amount. But I'm telling you, Laurel is a bridezilla. She won't let me have colored hair at the wedding. She wants me to dye it a 'respectful', her words, 'light *brunette* color'. In other words, don't look like my identical *blonde*! Twin! Sister!" Everyone on the other side of the pool turned their heads at Linda's shouting.

"Hey, you're shouting." Mason said.

"Am not. I'm speaking in all caps."

"All right. Take the caps lock off. Stat."

Linda huffed out a breath. "It would be one thing if she asked me to go natural, back to blonde, but I'd look too much like the bride, so she can't have that. She asked me to dye it brown."

"Hey." Mason sat up and leaned towards her. "You would be a gorgeous brunette. Just saying. Sounds like you need to chat with Laurel. But personally, I think you should go with whatever hair color you want. It's your head."

"It is my head. Thanks for that."

"Your pretty head."

"What's the flattery for, Mace?"

"It's not flattery. I'm trying to compliment you. Hoping to cheer you up. Guess it's not working." He leaned back on the lounge chair, crossed his arms and brought one finger up to his chin and began tapping in an exaggerated "thinking" gesture.

He started muttering to himself. "Hmmm, no." He paused and whispered, "Got it!" Then shook his head no. "Well, there's... would that work?"

Linda laughed. "Cut it out. I'm fine. It was a mild rant."

"Still worried about the work project?" he asked.

"I am."

"I'm sorry about that. Do you want me to call your boss and tell him I kept you from getting it done on time? Would that help?"

She smiled at him. "Thank you for offering, but no. It was my responsibility. I was having such a great time, I lost track of time. I should have been mindful. Just stop being so charming, will ya?"

"All right, all right, but I can be your punching bag if you need it. My offer to apologize to your boss still stands if you change your mind."

"I'll keep it in mind."

He lowered his ball cap to sit right above his sunglasses. "If I fall asleep, don't let me get sunburned."

"I got your back. Or your front. Whatever."

She shook her head, embarrassed at her statement. Not like she was watching his chest rise and fall.

Opening the cooler, she searched for a Coke. Two in one day was unusual for her, but she needed the shot of cold, sugary goodness.

What was she thinking, hanging out with Mason like this? Like they were *friends* and not exes.

Between her frustration with herself over missing the proposal deadline and irritation with her sister's wedding demands, Linda was thankful that Mason was here and trying to cheer her up. He'd charmed his way into her heart twice before, and her heart was softening towards him again.

Mason closed his eyes, replaying Linda's reaction to his invitation to be his date for Laurel's wedding over and over in his mind.

If he was honest, it was crushing. He knew it was too soon to suggest it, but he didn't like seeing Linda upset and feeling like she had to dull her shine for her sister.

He couldn't nap while Linda was still upset about everything. This might keep her miffed, but he had to know. He turned so he could watch her reaction to this next question. "Operation Keep Laurel Happy is underway," Mason began. "My apologies for not taking your sister's needs into account. You're right. People would talk if we went together. They would say 'There goes the cutest couple here', besides the bride and groom, of course. So, who are you taking? Someone I know? Someone from our college crowd?"

Linda scrunched her nose; he loved the way she did that. "No. It won't be anyone you know. Don't worry."

"I'm not." Didn't matter if it was someone he knew or not. He wasn't worried so much as jealous.

"Who will you ask?" she asked, her voice hushed and uncertain. Did she not want him to take someone? What did that mean?

"I don't have a go-to date for weddings. I don't know who I could ask. If I meet someone at my next job who would take a flight and hang out in Illinois for a couple of days, it would be a stroke of luck. As it is, I'll have..." he pretended to look at a watch on his watchless arm, "...less than two months to find someone, charm them, and get them to go with a near-stranger to a wedding. Totally doable." He chuckled. "I'll probably go stag."

"I'm sure you'll have no problem." Linda picked up the book she'd brought and opened it. She took the pink bookmark out and tapped its edge against her thigh.

Mason knew he should drop the conversation, but he forged ahead.

"If I bring someone, will you promise to be nice to her?" he asked.

Linda paused for a few moments before answering. "I promise," she said.

I'm an idiot. Why did he even ask the question? Trying to see if it would make her jealous? She didn't seem jealous; she seemed hurt. No way was he taking a date to Laurel's wedding! He hoped she wouldn't, either. Then they could hang out together. It wouldn't be weird if they weren't on a date.

Maybe he should just shut up and let her read. No, had to push his luck. "Promise me one dance at the wedding, whether or not we bring dates?"

Her head spun around. "Seriously? We're negotiating dances?"

"Not negotiating. Just asking for a yes, in advance."

"Fine. I promise."

Good. He had that to look forward to.

Now, how could he cheer her up? Flowers? Too romantic. Chocolate? She wasn't overly fond of chocolate. Hmmm.

"Are Skittles still your favorite candy?"

"Absolutely."

"Cool."

He had an idea.

Chapter 15

Mason told Linda about the fireworks at the condo building next door as they went back in. He suggested they go to dinner, stroll up and down the beach, and get back in time for fireworks.

She agreed to fireworks only, saying she needed time in the evening to work on a new project for her boss. That was true, but she would be done with the new project in less than thirty minutes. She needed some non-Mason time to work through the conflicting emotions that had been coursing through her ever since he'd suggested they go to Laurel's wedding together.

The idea was preposterous. Weddings were one of the most romantic events you could attend. They were full of hope and dreams and sprinkled with wishes and joy. It was hard to protect your heart at a wedding, and that's what Linda needed to do. Protect her heart from Mason.

When he'd broken up with her last time, he'd tossed her heart aside like moldy bread, when she'd decided he was her soulmate. She would have followed him anywhere in the world if he'd asked her. She saw their future together vividly. Their house, what cars they'd drive, and how many kids they'd have. She was excited and fired up about that future with Mason.

And then he'd said he needed to go. Alone. She'd cried for hours and wondered if she needed to go to prompt care for her heart palpitations and shortness of breath.

Devastation had consumed her. Once he'd left, she'd collapsed on her bed and hadn't moved until her sister had stopped by the following evening.

The sight of Laurel on her doorstep unleashed a new flood of tears, but like a good big sister, Laurel had wiped her tears, brought her ice cream, and hugged her until Linda could smile again. The sadness slowly faded away, leaving her feeling adrift, like Rose on the door in the *Titanic* movie.

She hit send on the email to Grady that included her research on a commercial property in downtown Normal. Even distracted with thoughts of Mason, she knew her research was thorough and exactly what Grady was looking for.

Moving to the couch, she typed a text message to Sorcha.

Linda: Can you talk?

A few seconds later, Sorcha called.

"Hey, Lulu. What's up?" Sorcha said.

"Hi! I had some downtime; thought we could catch up. How are things going?" She pulled her legs under her and leaned on a large throw pillow to get comfortable.

"Wonderfully. Living the dream. How are things going there with Mason?" The way Sorcha drew out his name made Linda laugh.

"Things are fine. We've been volunteering together this week, so I'm spending a bunch of time with him. I feel like I'm getting the closure I needed."

"Oh, yeah? Tell me more."

"Things are nice. Comfortable. I think we will come out of this as friends again."

"Friends?"

"Yes, just old family friends," Linda said. "Nothing more."

"Uh, huh." Sorcha was not buying it.

"Simply friends," Linda insisted. "Hey, I was thinking about Wyatt again. Do you honestly think he might be interested in me?"

"Duh. Yeah." Sorcha's eye roll was evident, even over the phone. "I've told you that a dozen times. You think you might hit him up when you get back?"

"Yeah. I think I will. I'm going to have to make sure I have a date for Laurel's wedding. There's no way I'm flying solo. Mason will be there. And I think he's bringing a date."

"And that's okay, because the two of you are friends..."

"Right! It's okay, but I still don't want to be dateless. Even if Mason wasn't going to be there, but it's an added incentive."

"Yeah, yeah. Whatever. But when you get home, we'll go and say hello to handsome Wyatt. You'll have to drop a hint or two that you're interested, because you've acted oblivious so far. He may have given up on you looking his way."

"Great. I'm home a week from Sunday."

"That's too long. I miss my roomie."

"Same."

"What are you doing this weekend?"

"Meri gave us tickets to the festival that we've been volunteering for." Linda stretched her legs out. They were cramping. "We're going on Saturday. Tomorrow, I'm going to drive to Tampa and check out a few stationery stores. Hoping to get some inspiration for new printables. No plans after Sunday. And one more week to relax, spend time on the beach."

"Sounds amazing."

"Right. I think I should set a goal, though..."

"You and your goals. Can't you relax?"

"Not really. I think my goal will be two new printable designs each day, Sunday through Saturday. With a stretch goal of twenty total for the week."

"That sounds like a lot for someone on vacation."

"I know, but it feels doable."

Linda looked out the patio doors. The sun was setting, and the sky was lit up with pink and purple streaks. The clouds seemed extra fluffy and happy. If Linda wasn't careful, she'd thoroughly enjoy the evening and the fireworks.

When Linda answered the door, Mason couldn't catch his breath for a moment. She'd curled her hair into soft waves around her face, applied dramatic purple eye makeup, and had on a light purple long-sleeved T-shirt that made her blue eyes pop.

She was always beautiful, with or without makeup, but when she took extra time getting ready, as he could tell she had, she was stunning.

She had a tote bag hanging on her shoulder and said she was ready to go as soon as she opened the door.

Linda brought the "sand-proof" beach blanket and Mason brought a cooler of assorted cold beverages. He was looking forward to sleeping in on Friday morning, his first opportunity all week.

Since they were crashing the party, Mason suggested they set up their blanket about twenty yards away from the crowd. They could see the fireworks and hear the music that was being pumped through large speakers but wouldn't be in the way of the residents.

Once they found a spot for the blanket, Linda asked, "Do you want to sit on the right side or left side?"

Mason glanced around. "If they are shooting off the fireworks directly in front of their building, why don't I sit on the left side, since I'm taller?"

"Makes sense."

Linda sat down and opened the cooler. "What did you bring?"

Mason caught a whiff of her shampoo as he sat next to her. He imagined putting an arm around her and pulling her close but resisted the urge. "I have a few IPAs and a couple of light beers and a few seltzers. Take whatever you want."

She reached in and grabbed a seltzer. "Can I get something for you?"

"Yes, an IPA. I have koozies in the front pocket if you want one."

Mason took the beer from Linda. She'd put it in a koozie with the Miami Dolphins logo on it.

"Cheers," she said, holding her can towards him.

"Cheers, Lindy. Thanks for coming out with me tonight. I might have felt like a dweeb out here by myself."

Linda looked towards the water. "Don't you have lots of experience going into crowds alone? Since you move so frequently, I mean."

"You're right." Her words poked at the loneliness that followed him like the cloud of dust that follows the Pigpen cartoon character. "I do." He half shrugged. "I don't mind being somewhere I don't know anyone. I take a few minutes to survey the crowd and look for friendly faces, then I introduce myself. Easy-peasy."

"Wow. I can't imagine. I've lost my ability to strike up conversations like that. Haven't really done that since college. Everything is transactional now. I say hi to people I interact with and chit-chat, but I'm not good at making friends. I have my circle and can fill up my social slots each week. I guess I don't have very many available slots. I like to work, watch movies, and read. I'm a simple person."

"You're not simple," he replied. "You're complex, and you have a lot of interests. Look, you went parasailing the other day. That's daring. I've never done that. Now I want to. If I can make reservations next week, would you go back with me?"

"Heck, yes!" Linda's eyes glowed.

Mason checked his watch. The fireworks should start soon. Looking out at the Gulf, he watched a large ship move north. It was too far away to make out more than its large shape and a few windows.

It would be nice to take a boat ride with Linda. Maybe he'd look for an excursion to do with her. They were both going to be there for another week. He was thankful none of their other family members were around. It was great having so much one-on-one time with her.

Mason chuckled. "See. You're daring. Few people would try parasailing. So what if you're not all that social? That's okay. It doesn't make you simple."

"Are you sure?" Her voice was soft and uncertain.

"One hundred percent positive. Hey, did you hear back about the deadline issue from work yesterday?"

"No." Her eyes were steady and her voice was resolute.

"Shoot. Sorry I brought it up. I didn't mean to bum you out."

"You're not. I'm not stressing over it. It was a mistake, not a crime. Not that I'm being flippant about it. I have high standards for myself, and I hated to disappoint Grady. But he's reasonable. Even if he loses out on the opportunity because of my mistake, he'll take it in stride and move on." She paused and leaned into Mason. "After he gives me three tongue lashings to make sure I've learned my lesson."

Linda's light blue eyes were so close he could see the dark outer ring of blue. He wanted to lean even closer and search for freckles on her nose, but he restrained himself. "Serious?"

"No. I'm kidding!" She laughed. "I think he said his piece yesterday. He was clearly disappointed, but he won't continue to berate me over it. That's fair." She shrugged. "He's not one to keep bringing it up."

"That's good."

"Yeah, it is. That's why I enjoy my job so much. He's a great boss."

Mason hated hearing her admiration for her boss. He imagined the guy walking around in three-piece suits, dressed like a billionaire, with thick, slicked-back dark hair. He probably drove a Maserati and vacationed in Europe. Mason didn't even know the guy, but he was starting to dislike him.

"I'm glad you like it. It makes me happy knowing you're in a good place in life."

"Oh, sure. I'm in a great spot," she said, dripping sarcasm. "My sister is getting married in two months, and I'm not in a relationship, but other than that, it's fabulous."

"Do you want a relationship?"

She took a long sip of her drink instead of answering him. After a few moments, she shrugged and looked towards the crowd. "Think the fireworks will start soon?"

She wouldn't answer his question; that shrug did not count as an answer. He'd hit a sore spot. Maybe it was too soon for them to talk about relationships, when he'd been the one to ruin theirs.

A large boom sounded, and a flash of light rocketed skyward. The fireworks were being launched from the edge of the water, going almost straight up. They were launching towards the water to reduce the risk of someone getting burned, which Mason was happy to see. He didn't want to have to launch into nurse mode and leave Linda's side.

Tonight was for having fun with Linda. And they had been having fun until he'd brought up the relationship thing. He'd have to move their conversation into a safer realm soon.

Linda was thankful for the fireworks. She did not want to discuss her relationship status with Mason. There was no status. And if she didn't watch her heart, it could let him back in again.

Unfortunately, the fireworks display only lasted for ten minutes. She oohed and aahed with the rest of the crowd, but her brain was tallying a list of all the reasons she couldn't fall under Mason's spell again.

First, she had no intention of living life out of a suitcase like Mason. Even though her job gave her location flexibility, she had cats to care for, and they loved home. She hoped they were enjoying their time at Laurel's. She needed to call and check on them. Probably needed to talk to Laurel about the wedding and bridal shower plans, too. She added that phone call to her mental to-do list.

Secondly, she'd never seen a successful long-distance relationship, and that's what theirs would be, at least for a while. He was leaving for somewhere else in a week, and she was heading home. That wouldn't work.

Last, even if, and it was a big if, he would move back to Illinois so they could pursue a relationship, what would prevent him from leaving again?

Not only had Mason left, but her last serious boyfriend, Brent, had left as well. He was the last guy who'd made it past three dates. They'd gone out for a couple months. She had let her guard down, and then he announced he was moving back home to Pennsylvania. Luckily, she'd never told him she loved him, so it didn't hurt as badly as Mason leaving but even though it had been over three years, the hurt still stung.

The fireworks ended, and there was a healthy round of applause. Linda set her drink down to join in. As others started to stand and gather their things, Linda looked to Mason to see if he was ready.

He was looking at the water and hadn't moved. She wondered if he'd even watched the fireworks. He had a melancholy look about him.

Against her better instincts, she reached out and put her hand on his forearm. The heat from his skin seemed to spark against her fingertips.

"Mason? Are you okay?" she asked, leaning towards him.

"Hmm?" he asked, shaking his head and turning to look at her.

She smiled a half-smile. "Did you notice the fireworks ended?"

"Oh, that's what the clapping was for." He smiled and nodded.

"What's wrong?" This was not normal behavior for him. He'd been happy and upbeat before the fireworks started. Up until she didn't respond to the relationship comment.

"Sorry. I was thinking about a patient. The last thing we'd talked about was his plans for the Fourth of July. He couldn't wait to see the fireworks."

Mason dropped his head.

"Oh, did he leave the hospital before you could say goodbye?" She could see Mason wanting to see his patients before they left.

"No." Mason didn't look up. "He died."

Linda inhaled sharply. That was not what she expected. "Mason, I'm sorry."

She put an arm across his shoulders and leaned into him, letting him know she was there to support him.

He lifted his head and took a drink of the beer in his hand. "I thought it would get easier," he whispered.

Linda's heart squeezed. She hated to see him hurting. She remembered how crushed he'd been when his mom died. His sister Erin had called her to come and comfort Mason because no one else could. Linda rushed to his home to hold him. They lay on his bed for hours as he cried, and she held him. Hours of murmuring that it was going to be okay. Hours of rubbing his back and saying, "I'm here, Mason."

She could do this again. She could comfort him as a friend. "But if grief was easy," she said, "would you be the caring, generous, loving person you are?"

Mason sighed. "Wow. I didn't expect that. Thank you."

Linda wondered how long Mason had been bottling up this sadness. She thought it would help if he talked about it. "Tell me about this person who wanted to see the fireworks."

Mason leaned his head back and she could see his eyes searching the stars. "Bradley. Ten years old. Leukemia. Smart kid. Loved to talk about space. He'd grill me on the planets and stars. He was always reading books about space. And in the end, his parents read to him constantly. Like they worried the moment they stopped reading, he'd stop listening. Broke my heart. I don't plan to do another child oncology stint again, if I can help it."

"Oh, Mason. That is so sad. I'm sure the kid and his family appreciated having you there."

He turned towards her. "Thanks. I hope I didn't bring you down too much. Did you enjoy the fireworks?"

"I did. I wish you could have."

"Hey, don't worry. I did." He reached for her hand, and she let him hold it. "Thankful to be here with you tonight."

His voice had grown softer, or maybe the crowd had thinned out. Or maybe both. Linda was more aware of the sound of the surf hitting the shore and the chill in the air. She shivered.

"Here. Take my sweatshirt." Mason handed her his hoodie. She grabbed it eagerly and pulled it over her head.

When she emerged, cozy within the warmth of the heavy material, Mason was leaning towards her. His eyes searched hers and her pulse quickened. *He's going to kiss me! What do I do?*

Mason leaned closer and his hand reached towards her face. To her dismay, he didn't touch her face or brush his lips to hers. Instead, he pulled on the hood of the sweatshirt and smoothed it behind her.

"It was crooked," he said, pulling away.

"Thanks," she squeaked out between constricted throat muscles. She didn't want him to kiss her, so why did she feel so disappointed?

Chapter 16

Mason asked Linda to join him on a catamaran cruise in the gulf on Friday, but she declined. She needed some distance to evaluate the almost kiss and her reaction to it. Besides, she planned to drive to Tampa and check out a few stationery stores, hoping to find inspiration for new designs for her Etsy storefront.

Walking into the first shop, "Plan to Succeed!", Linda thought the exclamation mark was a little over the top. Nothing added to the anxiety of someone wanting to succeed like the stress caused by that piece of punctuation. Her own brain was shouting at her to stay productive; she didn't need the store name to do the same.

Linda was the only customer in the store and felt she was on a hidden camera. There was a small black yorkie puppy following her everywhere. Whenever she paused to look at merchandise, it would put its front paws on her leg and jump up and down until she petted it.

The clerk behind the counter kept calling for the pup, "Come here, Pudding!", to no avail. It continued to follow Linda closely.

Feeling guilty browsing, she picked up a cute picture frame with "Newlyweds" written in a fancy font along the bottom. She'd give it to Laurel for her shower. She had access to their engagement photos and would get one to fill the frame. Laurel would likely replace it with a wedding photo, which was fine by Linda.

At the register, she chatted with the young woman, who finally enticed Pudding back behind the counter by offering a rawhide bone.

She hopped in the car and drove fifteen minutes to the next shop on her list. On the way, her mind kept replaying the conversation with Mason. It warmed her heart that he'd opened up to her about the loss of his young patient. She hated to see him so sad and briefly wondered if she should suggest he change careers. But his compassion made him who he was. It was probably his greatest quality. And she couldn't think of another role that would allow him to share his compassion with others more.

Replaying the moment when she'd thought he might kiss her over in her mind, she was confused. She was certain she wasn't putting out "I might be interested" vibes. Was it just that he was sad and seeking comfort? Probably.

That was good. Right? He shouldn't be interested in her. They weren't in the right place to rekindle anything. She hoped they would come out of this as friends again, that's all. But a small part of her felt disappointed. She was shocked to realize she'd wanted him to kiss her. When he leaned towards her, her eyes fluttered, and she wanted to turn over her senses to feel his lips on hers.

"Ugh! Stop it!" she shouted to herself as she pulled into the parking lot of "Polly's Papers."

Inside the store, she was greeted by a woman who was drying her hands on a towel as she walked out of a backroom with a beaded curtain doorway.

"Howdy!" she called. "Welcome. I'm Polly!" She walked towards Linda and stuck out her hand.

Linda shook the offered hand. "Hi, Polly. I'm Linda. What a cute store you have!"

Her eyes glanced around the room, which some might say was an overload of colors and graphics, but Linda loved the colorful, chaotic space. Products stuffed every shelf. There were brightly colored baskets holding oodles of sticker sheets, bookcases stuffed with books and journals, rows and rows of fancy ink pens (even a few feather quills!), and a display of various inks.

It was everything Linda loved about paper and designs.

"Thank you, dear," Polly responded. "I make some items myself."

"Really? Like what?"

Polly walked towards a wall of shelves filled with stacks of T-shirts. Linda noticed that the woman walked with a slight limp. "I design these and do all the silk-screening myself. That's what I was doing when you came in. I have a studio in the back."

Linda's eyes roved over the bright, comical shirts. She saw a couple that she knew she would purchase before leaving. The "Always the Bridesmaid, Never the Bride" with the face of an overly sad young woman caught her eye first. Laurel's wedding would be the fourth time she'd be a bridesmaid, and her first time as maid of honor, so it felt fitting.

"They're awesome! Clever and bright. Catchy."

"Thank you. What brings you in today? How can I help?" Polly asked, tucking the towel in the back pocket of her cargo pants.

"I'm browsing. Looking for inspiration." Linda worried the words might be misconstrued as soon as she said them. She wasn't looking to steal someone's ideas.

"Oh? Are you an artist?"

"No. Not a real artist. I make designs and templates using some tools. I can't draw to save my life. A teacher once laughed at me when I drew a horse; she said it looked like a camel. So embarrassing. Luckily it was May, so we were out of school shortly after. Took me all summer to draw again."

"Ouch. Shame on that teacher. You should never tease kids about stuff like that. What do you design?"

"Printables. Templates that people can download. I sell them on Etsy. You know, things like invitations, party games, to-do lists. That sort of thing." Linda picked up a bright yellow pad of paper that had a drawing of a frog on a pond leaf that read, "I'm going to hop to it and get these things done today! Ribbit!"

She smiled. "Things like this. But the person who buys it prints it out themselves or does it digitally."

"I see." Polly nodded. She pulled the towel out of her pocket and dusted a shelf. "That's interesting. I've seen those things online. But I like the touch and smell of paper too much to keep a digital list. I love writing it out longhand and then putting a big check mark when I get something done. Nothing more satisfying than that."

"I'm the same. I love journaling and writing longhand. Just don't ask me to draw. Speaking of, I could use a new journal." She swung her head, looking for where they would be.

"Over here." Polly led the way to a revolving display of beautiful glossy and embroidered hardback journals. "There are these, and then I have some spiral ones on that back bookcase. Regular paper ones on that shelf over there."

"Perfect." Linda spun the display and found a cute journal with a pink owl wearing purple glasses on it. "I love this one." She tucked it under her arm and went back to the T-shirt display, grabbing two.

Polly ambled back to the counter and sat on a rattan stool. "Ah. Time for a break." She reached below the counter and pulled out a large tumbler covered in stickers.

Linda watched Polly out of the corner of her eye. The woman had white hair cut in a bob, and there were shiny strands of purple in it. Ah, *fairy hair. Cool.* For living in Florida, she thought Polly's skin was extra creamy, like she avoided the sun, or had a great handle on sunscreen.

Polly wore a loose chambray shirt, light blue, with the sleeves rolled up to her elbows. There was no jewelry on her hands or wrists, but she had dangling silver earrings that tinkled when she moved her head, and a long silver chain with a glass circle pendant hung around her neck. Linda wondered if the pendant was handmade. She glanced around, thinking there might be some jewelry displayed, but she didn't see any.

Taking her purchases to the counter, she asked Polly how long she'd been in business.

"Twenty years. Started in a smaller location but was able to expand and move here twelve years ago."

"Do you love owning your own store?" Linda asked.

"I do. Love being my own boss. Deciding what to sell. When to be open. Meeting customers. My grandson helped me set up an online store a year ago." She pulled a business card out of a plastic holder that read "I love Tampa" on the front. "Here. You can shop from me even when you're not close. Do you live in Florida?"

"No. I'm on vacation. Staying at my uncle's condo in Seaside Bay. I'm from and live in central Illinois. Bloomington."

As Linda watched Polly ring up her purchases and bag them, she pulled her wallet out of her purse. Rifling through her cash, she hoped she wouldn't need to use a credit card. She preferred to use cash for small businesses; she knew how the credit card fees ate into one's profits.

"Having a good vacation?"

Linda thought about Mason. It was a resounding yes, so she said so. Would it have been as good if Mason hadn't shown up? Definitely not.

"That's good. Here you go." Polly handed her a paper shopping bag with a stamped image of the store's logo on the front. Linda wondered if Polly printed them herself. "If you ever get to a point in your design career where you make physical products, reach out and let me know. Maybe I could carry your stuff in my store."

Linda paused. She'd never considered that before. Pulling out her phone, she quickly jotted a few notes. She would investigate print options, and perhaps she could find a few retailers at home to carry her original designs, too. "Thank you. I hadn't thought about doing that."

Polly nodded, her earrings' dulcet tones ringing softly. "I like to encourage young women entrepreneurs. Part of my giving back. I wish there had been more around when I started out. Got to pay it forward; remember that."

"I agree. Oh, here." Linda searched in her purse for her business card. "Here's the name of my Etsy storefront. If you get a chance, look and see if there are any items that you think would sell well in your store. Maybe those will be the first that I'll consider having made and selling wholesale."

"I'll check it out."

Linda walked out of the store filled with something that she hadn't come for. Inspiration for a whole new line of business. She had a few new ideas for designs — frogs were in her future — which is what she'd come in for. But Polly's idea of selling wholesale was new to Linda.

"Huh," Linda said to herself as she popped the trunk to put in her bag. She glanced across the parking lot and saw a food truck selling tacos. Her stomach growled; she hadn't eaten breakfast before she'd left the condo. Time for lunch.

Glancing back at Polly's store, she thought, *What if I opened my own retail store? I'd get to look at, buy, and recommend the things I love the most.* She shook her head. *Don't get too far ahead of yourself. That would cost a fortune to start. You don't have that kind of money. Besides, it would be a colossal risk. Best just to think about expanding to physical products. A safer bet.*

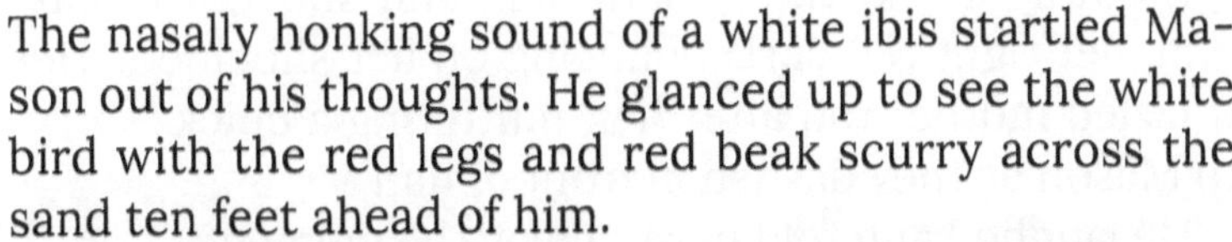

The nasally honking sound of a white ibis startled Mason out of his thoughts. He glanced up to see the white bird with the red legs and red beak scurry across the sand ten feet ahead of him.

The noise and movement shook the cobwebs from his mind.

"Move along," he called to the bird, thankful no one was around to hear him.

He was cooling down from his jog, walking back towards the condo building. Covered in sweat, he was looking forward to a cool condo and an even cooler shower.

He'd felt disappointed when Linda said she had things to do today and would not be available. *It's fine.* He could use the time to research Seattle, Washington and Portland, Maine, to help him decide where to move next.

He'd done that research first thing this morning, even jotting down a few notes for a pro/con list. He tried to tell himself he *hadn't* already decided on Seattle while researching. But once Linda had said she'd like to visit there someday, a tiny part of him knew that's where he was going next.

If there was the slightest chance that he could get her to visit him, he would. He wanted to spend as much time with her as possible. He was fairly confident that they had worked their way back to being friends again. With additional time together, he hoped they could be even more.

Spending time with her this week had reminded him of everything that made her such a wonderful person. Her diligence, creativity, laughter, and kindness to others were at the top of the list of reasons he had fallen in love with her before. Time hadn't changed those aspects of her personality, only strengthened them.

If he was in Seattle for twelve weeks and she visited him once, and he went back to Illinois once, they could stay connected and continue to strengthen their relationship.

A young girl with a plastic pail and shovel ran past him, her tight red curls bouncing on her shoulders. Her frazzled mother ran after her, muttering a quick "sorry" to Mason as they dashed in front of him.

He laughed and told her to enjoy the moment.

Continuing on his way, he rethought his day. He should have swapped tasks around and taken his run *before* internet surfing. He would have saved himself from sweating a pound of water out of his body if he'd run when it had been cooler outside.

"Now what am I going to do?" he muttered to himself, glancing at his watch. It was only noon. He had a full afternoon and evening to fill.

He shouldn't complain. He hadn't expected to have someone to hang out with this week, anyway. Or the chance to volunteer for Meri. Why was he so anxious now with a day unscheduled, when he thought he'd have two weeks of them?

Finally getting back to the condo, he popped his head into Meri's office. He couldn't find her and realized she was probably at the Blueberry Festival.

Back in the condo, he showered and put on fresh clothes. Sitting on the couch, he pulled out his phone.

He wanted to text Linda, but didn't want to bother her. Thinking of Linda made him think back to the fireworks.

He'd been as shocked as she had when he told her about the kid who passed away from cancer.

Normally, he could keep work challenges like that—losing a patient, a patient taking a turn for the worse, being unable to save a limb, or whatever other setback occurred—bottled up. Safely stored in the lockbox called 'bad work stuff.' He'd shove all pain or heartache from work in there, lock it up, and push it way back under the imaginary bed. Unlike his dad and sister, he rarely talked about the things that went wrong at work. He only wanted to talk about successes: the healing, the cures, and the recoveries.

But last night with Linda, it felt different. Safe. She wouldn't judge him for grieving a patient; he'd known that instinctively. And she hadn't. When she validated his feelings and comforted him, a giant weight had released from his shoulders. It was as though Linda had taken that lockbox out from under the bed and thrown it into an active volcano—it was good and gone, no worries that it would come back.

At that moment, he had ached to kiss her. He'd wanted to lean over and be close enough to relax in her orbit, caress her face, and inhale the scent of her.

He'd pushed the urge down. He was sure she would have rejected him, and as vulnerable as he was feeling at that moment, it would have crushed him.

Trying to divert his mind from Linda, he scrolled the contacts in his phone. He needed to talk to someone. Ask if he was crazy for wanting to pursue the girl who'd always held that special place in his heart. That place reserved for first and last loves. So rare that the same person could fill both spaces, but Mason was sure she could, and he hoped she would.

More time. She needs more time. Be patient.

He saw the names of several buddies he'd met at various hospitals around the country. It was cool to see the geographical variety of people. But they were acquaintances, not close friends.

The last good friend he'd had, Kellen, was from high-school. They'd tried keeping in touch during college, but Kellen attended school in Iowa and moved to California once he graduated.

They'd met up once a few years before, when Mason was living in Anaheim. They'd had dinner, a few beers, caught up on work and families, and parted ways.

That was the problem with changing jobs and cities so frequently. He didn't build strong relationships.

By design. It was easier to move on and not get attached. Leave before they could leave you, through falling out, breaking up, or even worse, by dying, like his mom.

Losing Bradley had knocked him for a loop. It was always rough losing a patient, but losing a kid was the worst.

Sometimes he needed someone to lean on, to vent to. Times when a workout or a jog didn't expel the pain and hurt caused by the job. Times when he needed a friend to listen and encourage him.

That's what he needed. Stronger relationships. That needed to start with his dad, sister, and stepmom. For too long, he'd treated them too casually, taking family for granted. Assuming they'd be there for him; family had to be.

But did they?

If he wasn't putting in the time, phone time and face time, why should they? Were they feeling how much he loved and appreciated them?

Sighing, he reached for a pad of paper on the coffee table. He wrote a simple list. Dad, Erin, Linda, old friends, new friends. He had a lot of work to do. But now that he knew what to focus on, it would be easy to take action.

Maybe Linda will be up for dinner, he thought. He texted her that question, but she quickly replied with "Sorry, can't. Busy. See you tomorrow. Ten am to go to fest?"

He replied affirmatively and tossed his phone across the couch. Her rejection intensified his loneliness. He couldn't blame her, but it was further proof how much work he had to do.

Grabbing the condo keys, he left. He was going to the grocery store to buy several large bags of Skittles and a basket to hang on the door to her condo. He imagined her smile when she found it, and smiled himself as he punched the button for the elevator.

He would also go to a hardware store to find a smart thermostat. He needed something to keep his mind occupied for the rest of the day. Once he installed it, he would call his dad to let him know. Then he'd call Erin to see how she was doing.

Chapter 17

Carnival games lined the festival midway. They were never a big attraction for Linda, as they made her feel like she wasn't clever enough, strong enough, or fast enough to win a prize.

What she lacked in enthusiasm, Mason made up for in his desire to try everything at least once. Taking a swing of the hammer on the high-striker strongman game, he won a prize, an eighteen-inch-tall gorilla with a white Blueberry and Blues Festival shirt.

"I can't believe you won something!" Linda bopped the gorilla on the nose as Mason showed it to her.

"I got skills, Lindy! What can I say?"

"Say you're not going to make me carry that around. It's ninety degrees out here. Too hot to carry around a stuffed animal."

He nodded. "That's right. Hold on." He scanned the crowd and saw a young boy who was crying. He went over to the boy and his mom and said a few words, Linda was too far away to hear. The young boy broke out into a huge smile when Mason handed him the gorilla. The mom thanked Mason profusely before he rejoined Linda.

"There, no gorilla to deal with," he said.

Linda leaned up and kissed him on the cheek. "My hero," she drawled. "That was sweet of you."

He shrugged. "What was I going to do with it? I won it to show off for you. If you didn't want it, best to give it to a kid."

"Technically, I didn't say I didn't want it," Linda teased. "I just said I wouldn't carry it in this heat."

"What?" Mason put his hand to his heart. "Now you tell me! I would have carried it all day and all night for you."

Linda laughed at his antics, then turned to look at the next booth. She didn't want him to see the effect those words had on her. She was sure her cheeks were flushed red from kissing him!

"So, what did you do yesterday?" Mason asked as they strolled along.

"Research and shopping in Tampa."

"What kind of research?"

Linda pointed at a small food truck with a sign reading "Blueberry Ice Cream" on its side. "Ice cream?"

He nodded, and they stood in line.

After placing their orders and receiving waffle cones filled with two scoops of blueberry ice cream, Linda continued. "Research for my printables business. I was looking for design inspiration."

"Did you find some?"

"Yes. I'm going to do something with frogs."

Mason threw his head back and laughed. "That's wide open."

Linda smiled. "It is."

"Tell me more about this side hustle of yours. How did you get started?"

"Sorcha and I were complaining about our rent going up, and we started brainstorming ways to earn a little extra money. I had been experimenting with designing my own organization tools: to-do lists, shopping lists, planners, etc. and thought it would be a straightforward thing to try."

"Yeah."

"Easy to try, but difficult to execute at first. I had a lot to learn, but I kept at it, and I've had my storefront for a couple years now."

"It's profitable?"

"Yes, enough to take the pressure off when unexpected bills hit. And I'm happy to say that I committed to donating ten percent of all my profits to charity."

"Wow. That's...which charities?"

Linda took a moment before answering. She took a bite of ice cream to buy some time. She didn't want to trigger Mason's sadness.

"Some local organizations that support cancer patients." Before Mason could respond, she rushed forward. "There's a group that knits hats for patients going through chemo and another group that focuses on supporting the families, bringing food, driving patients to appointments, driving family members to school, that sort of thing."

"Amazing, Linda. That's admirable. Why cancer?"

She took a deep breath and blinked quickly to ward off the tears that threatened. "For your mom."

Mason held her eyes. He didn't smile or frown or anything. He looked stunned. Shifting his ice-cream cone to his left hand, he leaned towards her and hugged her with his right arm. He squeezed quickly and let go. "I know. I know. It's hot. But thank you. That's wonderful."

He looked towards the crowd moving towards the long strip of rides. Linda was thankful he'd shifted his gaze. If he'd held her gaze any longer, she would be crying.

"I love the idea of philanthropic entrepreneurship," she said. "I try to support other small businesses and charities that contribute to making the world a better place."

Mason turned back towards her. "Other than frogs, any other inspiration?" He was trying to lighten the mood, which Linda appreciated.

She took a bite out of the waffle cone. *Mmm, so good.* She considered his question. Yes, she was inspired to try some new products. And an itty-bitty idea was taking root in her soul.

Maybe she could open her own store. Yes, a large retail space would be challenging financially, but maybe she could start at farmers' markets or a co-op retail place.

There were options. She had spent hours the night before looking online and writing out a potential business plan. She wasn't ready to share that with Mason yet. Too much risk that putting the dream into words would tarnish its glow.

"Yes," she finally said. "I aim to make physical products, notepads to start. Then see if I can get some retail stores to carry my stuff. I talked to the owner of one store I went into yesterday, and she suggested it. I jotted down some notes last night. That's why I didn't go to dinner with you. We'll see what happens, but I'm excited about the possibilities."

"That's great! I want to look at your portfolio. Now and when you develop more."

"I'll send you the link to my Etsy store."

"Do that. You can do anything you set your mind to, Linda, you always have. I know you'll be successful with this. Never stop chasing your dreams!" Mason finished his cone and wiped his mouth with his napkin. "I feel refreshed. Ready to check out the rides?"

"The pie-eating contest starts in twenty minutes." She reached out and touched his arm. "Can we watch that first?"

"Yeah, sure thing."

Linda glowed with Mason's vote of confidence, even if others might confuse that glow with sweat. She wasn't the only one with beads of perspiration on her forehead, which she swiped at with an extra napkin, hoping it didn't leave little pieces of lint on her skin.

She could make a go of creating physical products. She would look for printing options next week and made a goal to set up a table at a farmers' market or vendor fair before the summer was out.

If she could prove to herself that there was a market for the things she wanted to make, she would look at further retail options this fall.

Excitement rippled through her like fast-moving waves under the skin. Raw energy and new ideas were competing for attention. She yearned for her journal so she could scribble the endless thoughts down.

She took a deep breath and looked down at her feet. She wiggled her toes in her tennis shoes, grounding herself in the here and now. Looking up at Mason, she felt a surge of emotions course through her. Thinking about his mom, feeling the love and loss of her, hearing his excitement about her ideas, and seeing his crooked smile, she wanted to throw her arms around him and hug him. But it was too hot. She pointed toward the pie-eating competition and said, "This way."

Mason couldn't talk Linda into any of the rides. She refused, saying they all looked like they were held together with zip ties. No, thank you.

They strolled the festival grounds, sampled blueberry bread, blueberry pie, blueberry custard, and blueberry tarts. Mason worried his teeth were going to be stained permanently blue before the day was over.

But it didn't matter. He got to spend the whole day with Linda. She was relaxed and excited and things felt easy between them.

He caught her enthusiasm about expanding her side hustle. Amazed and proud that she donated a portion of her earnings to charity, he would step up his own financial support for charity. He gave blood every time a hospital or clinic asked or held a drive, but he could do more.

They were moving into a large tent where karaoke was being held, when Linda got a phone call from her sister.

"Tell her I said hello!" Mason shouted as Linda said hello. She raised a hand to him and shushed him.

"Laurel? What's wrong?" she said into the phone, her eyebrows stitching together tightly.

Mason put his hand on Linda's lower back to guide her out of the line of people entering the tent. He directed her to an empty bench, and they sat down.

"What? Your veil? Oh, no!" Linda said.

Mason raised his eyebrows. *Oh boy.*

"My cats? You're kidding." She paused, nodding her head.

Mason smiled to himself at her gesture; Laurel couldn't see the head nod.

"I'm so sorry, Laur'. I'll pay to replace it." She winced at Mason, and he wondered how expensive wedding veils were.

Linda murmured agreement several more times before saying goodbye and hanging up.

"That didn't sound fun," Mason said, trying to lighten the mood.

"That's an understatement. Laurel is livid. My cats tore up her veil."

"How does that happen?"

"Don't know. I didn't want to ask a lot of questions. Laurel was beside herself. Bride nerves."

Linda bit her lip and Mason reached out and took her hand, giving it a squeeze. "Deep breath. Don't stress."

"I know. But it's a four-hundred-dollar veil. And I already have a lot of expenses related to the wedding. Maybe now's not the time to think about expanding my business."

"Yes, it is. I'll help with the cost of the veil."

"No! Absolutely not. It's not your responsibility."

"I know that. But I want to help. Consider it my wedding gift to Laurel. Will she think I'm cheap if I get her a toaster for the wedding?" Mason smiled, pleased when Linda smiled, too.

"She has a hundred-dollar toaster on her registry."

"What in the world?"

Linda laughed. "It's a toaster oven, you can bake a pizza in it, too."

"Wow. I need one of those. No, I don't. It would take up too much space in my suitcase." He grinned at her, but the smile fell from her face.

Idiot. Don't remind her you travel all the time.

"All righty. I'll find the cheapest thing on the registry."

"Good luck. She's got expensive tastes."

"Let's forget veils and registries and go sing karaoke."

Linda gave a deep sigh. "Sure. Duet?"

"Always. 'You're the One That I Want'?"

"Yep."

Two hours later, they left the karaoke tent and found the sun had set. The lights from the festival prevented them from seeing any stars, but Mason knew they were there. He wanted to take a walk on the beach when they got back to the condo building. He hoped Linda would be up for it.

Walking towards the parking lot, they found a large crowd of people leaving at the same time. Linda gave him a mischievous look and took off running. "Race you to the car!" she shouted over her shoulder.

Mason grinned and gave her a few more strides before he took off after her. He caught up to her a few yards from the car and ran past.

"Hey!" she yelled.

When he got to the car, he turned quickly and held out his arms. Not slowing down at all, she ran into him with full force.

"Oomph," he said as he took the impact of her body. Following her momentum, he picked her up and swung her around to keep from falling over. Setting her on the ground, he laughed and refused to let her go.

Her body shook with laughter, and she threw her head back. He impulsively leaned forward and kissed her lightly on her neck.

She shrieked and wriggled in his grasp, but she didn't break his grip. "Hey!"

"Hey, yourself. I won."

"You did." She stopped moving, and her eyes slid to his lips.

This was the moment he'd anticipated since watching fireworks with her. He didn't want to rush things, but he couldn't wait any longer. He leaned forward and kissed her.

Her lips were slightly salty and tasted like the popcorn they'd eaten earlier. He loosened his hold on her. If she wanted to break free, she could, but she remained in place. She kissed him back, slowly and gently, hesitant. She had every right to be cautious.

Much too soon, he broke the kiss and pulled back. He'd happily stand there for an hour kissing her, but he didn't want to frighten her away.

Everything about kissing her was just as he remembered it. Her lips, the way she felt in his arms, the flowery scent of her. Adrenaline coursed through him. As much as he enjoyed this moment, his chest felt hollow, the knowledge that he'd been the one to leave her six years ago heavy upon his heart.

How many kisses had he given up? How many times could he have held her in his arms? He'd given up so much more than he'd even realized in all his lonely nights.

"You okay?" he asked, pushing a strand of hair off of her face, his hand lingering on her shoulder. He resisted the urge to pull her to him again.

"Yes," she whispered, blinking slowly.

He kissed her on the nose and stepped back. There was so much he wanted to say, but words failed him.

He clicked the remote on the car and opened her door. "After you, Lindy."

Settling in the car, Linda let out a huff of air. "Whoa," she said softly once Mason shut her door.

She hadn't realized that he had hit the remote start. The air-conditioning was on full blast, and she shivered. A pleasant change from the scorching-hot day.

What just happened?

Challenging him to a foot race was apparently flirting, you fool. No wonder he kissed you.

I kissed him back, to be fair.

You did. Way to go!

Linda smiled to herself as Mason opened the driver's door. She'd hold all further self-talk, praise, admonishment, or other, until she was alone in the privacy of her uncle's condo again.

"Had a good day?" Mason asked, snapping on his seatbelt. She remembered to do the same.

"Almost perfect."

"Almost?" He put his hand on the headrest behind her and glanced all around the car before backing up. "What would have made it better?"

"Seeing you make a pig of yourself in the pie-eating contest," she teased.

"What? No way. That's a mess."

"Didn't say it wasn't."

Exiting the parking lot, Mason asked about her plans for Sunday.

"Hoping for a day of rest and relaxation. It was a hectic week. Much more so than I expected."

"R&R it is. Mind if I join you?"

Linda laughed. "Not at all."

How could she mind? Somewhere between the blueberry muffins and the blueberry ice cream, she'd forgiven him. He hadn't transformed into some cold, heartless monster when he left her six years ago. He'd been protecting his heart. Just what she'd been doing since he'd left.

No wonder she had a hard time dating a man more than a few times. If she left first, they couldn't beat her to it and hurt her. Protecting her heart, just as Mason had been protecting his heart from the grief that had nearly crushed him when his mom died.

Her heart felt lighter than it had in years. Happier. Today she'd felt like she was fifteen again, when the world was full of possibilities and opportunities. Her fifteen-year-old self would be proud that she was exploring the idea of expanding her business, willing to take on new risks. It was time to let go of list-building and start finger painting again.

Driving back to Seaside Bay, she watched the colors of the Gulf sunset shift from orange to pink to purple. *Frogs and sunsets, inspirations for my next designs.* She'd set her expectations low for this trip. A fun escapade with Sorcha, some downtime in Florida's sunshine, and a few new digital designs.

The events of the past week had surpassed her expectations. It seemed she had her friendship with Mason back, inspiration for a whole new side hustle—maybe a new career—and excitement about the future. This trip had already given her oodles more than she'd expected, and she still had a week remaining.

She paused. That kiss had been more than friendly. It alluded to new possibilities and third chances. Was she seriously considering trying again with Mason? How could they make it work if he was unwilling to move home? Should she consider moving? Would she? The excitement from the kiss wore off, and doubt crept back in.

Chapter 18

By Wednesday, Linda's tan was two shades deeper, the muscles in her face ached from laughing so much, and she'd designed two new series of templates based on Florida. She'd even drafted a one-page outline of her new business plan for producing and selling physical products. She felt great about where she was and where she was going, despite needing hours of additional research and development.

Though Mason asked, she didn't share too many details about the new product line. The idea needed more time to percolate. If she shared too much too soon, she was certain it'd flatten faster than a soufflé that had been over-mixed and cooked in a too-hot oven.

Once the sun zapped her energy, she told Mason she was showering to cool off. They'd spent two hours in the sun by the pool. Mason wanted to stay a little longer. They agreed to get together for dinner and a movie at Mason's place later that evening.

Entering the building, Linda took a left towards Meri's office instead of the elevator. She knocked lightly on the open door when it appeared that Meri was taking a siesta. Her head was down, resting on her folded forearms on the desk.

"Meri?"

Meridian jerked her head up and blinked rapidly. "Yes?"

"Sorry to disturb you." Linda hesitated. "Can I come in?"

"Linda! Hello!" Meri gestured for Linda to take a seat, then her hands went to her hair, and she smoothed the ends. She reached for her coffee cup, took a sip, and said, "Blech! It's gotten cold."

Meri stood, walked to the counter, and poured the offensive coffee in the sink. She refilled the cup and poured some powdered creamer into it. Linda wrinkled her nose, thankful that Meri's back was turned.

"What brings you in?" Meri asked.

"Wanted to chat with you for a minute, if you have time." Linda wanted to giggle, as she'd obviously woken Meri up from a nap.

"I can spare a few minutes." Meri turned and winked at Linda, playing along with the charade.

"If I run an idea by you, will you give me honest feedback?" Linda began.

Meri nodded as she walked back to her chair. "What's up?"

"Well, I have a side hustle—"

"What?"

"A side hustle. Something outside of my regular job. I design printables that people buy and download."

"Oh, I see. Go on." Meri opened a drawer and brought out a basket of mini chocolate bars. She held it out to Linda, who took a Twix.

"I want to expand my product line and have physical products to sell. With what I create, I see a potential market in gift shops, bookstores, and the like."

Meri nodded, tearing the wrapper off a Milky Way.

Linda continued. "I spoke to a business owner in Tampa the other day, and she said she would consider carrying my stuff."

"That's great!"

"Yeah. It is. My question, though..." Linda paused, gathering the nerve to put her big dream out into the universe. "I have an itch to open my own retail store. That's stupid, right?"

Meri's face twisted, and her eyebrows managed their own personal wave, like you see at baseball games. "Stupid?" She scoffed. "How you figure?"

"Well, it would cost a lot of money to start. I'd have to quit my day job to manage it. And there's no promise it would be successful." Linda threw her hands up in the air, telling herself it was a lost cause.

"Oh, hon, stop talking yourself out of it before you even begin! Stop the worrying, start the scurrying." Meri laughed at herself. "What I mean is, figure it out. Find the bite-size pieces," she said, holding up another mini chocolate bar, "like this! And move forward. How do you eat an elephant?"

"What?" Linda shook her head. "Who eats elephants?"

"You eat them, one bite at a time. It's a saying for when you get overwhelmed by all the things. You can only take one bite at a time. Focus on the little bites, and after a while, you'll have eaten an entire leg. Or something like that."

"Ah. What do you think about the idea of leaving my job? That's crazy, right? I have health insurance, a great boss, I like what I do..."

"Like? You like what you do? Right there is a reason to chase your dreams! Don't settle for doing something you *like* to do. Find something you're passionate about!" Meri sighed and leaned back in her chair. "Don't be like me," she mumbled, looking off into a distance at a life Linda couldn't even guess at.

The sigh Meri released spoke volumes about lost dreams and chances. Linda's heart squeezed in sympathy.

With another heavy sigh, Meri turned back to her and leaned forward, her finger tapping the desk to make her point. "Start small. Try things. Adjust. Try new things. Just keep going. Chase. That. Dream." Her finger pounded on each word.

Meri smiled broadly, and Linda couldn't help but do the same. "Thank you, Meridian. That was exactly what I needed to hear. Start small. But start. I'll figure it out."

"You will, dear. You will. Keep me updated."

"I will."

Linda stood and walked around the desk. She leaned over to give Meri a hug. "Thank you so much for believing in me."

"I believe, girl. I believe."

As much as Mason loved going out with Linda, to the festival, to dinner, for a walk on the beach, he loved being at the condo with her even more. Working together in the kitchen, preparing dinner, or cleaning up. Playing cards while they killed time indoors during the scorching afternoon. Or sitting in front of the TV, watching the news or a movie or some silly reality show. It didn't matter. He loved the time with her, talking, joking, and catching up on the past six years and exploring who they'd become.

Linda's newly discovered affinity for shows about stewards and deck hands on luxury yachts surprised Mason, but her newfound love of making crepes did not. She had always loved trying new recipes.

He often wondered it if was another way to distinguish herself from her twin. Laurel always whined about doing anything in the kitchen. She preferred playing outside over doing anything domestic.

He told Linda about the highs and lows of his experience as a nurse and as someone who roamed around the country, experiencing a variety of cultures, habitats, and cities. He showed her countless pictures of his various apartments. From his favorite, the "sky rise" in Boston, overlooking the Public Garden and the Charles River, to his least favorite, the "garden" apartment in Baltimore, the only garden view being the small pot of ivy he'd bought a week into his time there to have something green to look at.

When he moved, he took the plant to a patient in the hospital and wished both the plant and the patient a quick road to full recovery. (He'd found he wasn't the best caretaker for anything growing in soil.)

By Wednesday, he felt they'd made peace with their years apart. Their relationship was on a new, stronger foundation.

He didn't suggest again that they go to Laurel's wedding together, but it was always in the back of his mind. Linda was going. He was going. Why not go together? But after she'd soundly rejected that idea the week before, he knew to wait.

Once the dinner dishes were washed and drying in the rack, Linda ran back to her condo to grab a plate of cookies she'd baked earlier ("We won't eat dinner if I bring them before," she declared) and Mason dimmed the condo lights, opened the patio door to let fresh air in—the afternoon had brought a few rain showers and it had cooled significantly—and brought their glasses to the living room.

Linda let herself back in and he noticed she'd changed into the cute pajamas he'd seen her wearing that first morning on the balcony.

"Comfy?" he asked, as he leaned over to grab a cookie from the plate on the coffee table.

"Yes!" she answered brightly. "Ready to veg." She turned towards the patio door and took a few steps closer, inhaling deeply. "Ah, I love that smell."

Mason laughed and nodded. "Never gets old. Ready for a yachting marathon?"

"Aye, aye, Captain," she said, sitting and snuggling in close to him.

Four hours later, Linda was curled up on the large throw pillow on the opposite side of the couch, and his legs ached from sitting. He stood and glanced down at her. She was asleep.

He watched her face for a few seconds. The light from the TV cast a soft pink glow upon her features. The sun had brought out several freckles across her nose, and though he knew better than to mention them to her, he loved them. He wanted to count each one as he softly kissed them.

He hadn't kissed Linda since Saturday at the festival. He wanted to, but he felt a wall go up around her. Yes, she was fun and flirty, but cautious. He saw it in her eyes; she was wary. He'd asked if he'd offended her or pushed her away. She claimed her mind was crowded with new ideas for her business, but he wasn't convinced. He told himself to take it slow, but groaned, remembering they only had two more days together before he left for Seattle.

If they ended this week in the friend zone, that would be fine, but he worried that meant there couldn't be more.

He knew long-distance relationships were hard, but there were lots of examples of them working. He had few close friends, but he had several acquaintances in the traveling-nurse line of work; he'd seen both successes and failures in how they navigated their long-distance romances.

He had two more days to get an idea of where Linda's head was. Hopefully, she wasn't entirely preoccupied with work and had an opening for him in her heart.

When Linda awoke, she was lying on the couch with Mason's arms wrapped around her. Surprise washed over her, but she didn't feel alarmed. Being held by him filled her with peace.

The TV was on but muted, casting the only light in the room.

She remained still and closed her eyes against the light from the TV. A steady breeze blew in from the Gulf, the fresh scent wafting over her.

Mason's breathing alarmed her at first. He'd inhale deeply, exhale quickly, then not move for several seconds. But this pattern continued steadily, and she found it comforting once she was used to it.

She dimly remembered Mason shaking her lightly to ask her if she wanted to go to bed. She wasn't sure if he meant to go back to her own bed or go to his, and she didn't want to ask.

She shook her head, and he told her to stretch out on the couch before covering her in a light, soft throw. He'd gone to sit in the chair by the patio. She'd seen his silhouette there and wondered why she hadn't felt him crawl in behind her on the couch.

Must have been sound asleep.

Didn't matter. It felt nice. Her cheek was resting on his firm biceps, and she lifted her head to see if she'd sweated on him. She ran her hand over his upper arm and noticed the ridge of his muscle. No sweat. *That's good. Amazing arms. That's better.*

Her mind slowly played out the potential outcomes of this. If they woke up side by side on the couch, would it mean something? Would they kiss? Make out?

She couldn't do it, not a fleeting relationship. She wanted the long-term thing. She wanted endless nights falling asleep on the couch with him. Endless days working side by side around the house, fussing at each other in harmless fun. Endless hours of talking about their day, celebrating each other's successes and failures.

She wanted what they'd had before, the comfort and excitement of being in love with your best friend.

She was getting the friend part back, and as much as she hoped for more, she'd settle for that for now.

Moving slowly so she wouldn't wake him, she sat up and paused on the couch. He folded his arms at his side and sighed. That was a good sign. She stood up cautiously and grabbed her phone and two cookies. Late-night snack. She looked at the time: 3 a.m. Early morning snack.

She tiptoed out the door and back to her uncle's condo, eating the cookies as she went.

Back in her bedroom, she opened the patio door and took a deep inhalation of the cool, damp air. She wanted to bottle this smell and take it back to Illinois with her. The smell, the feeling, and Mason.

Chapter 19

Mason stepped into the elevator and shifted his backpack higher on his shoulder as he pulled the two rolling suitcases into place behind him. He punched the button for the first floor and watched as the doors closed.

Linda was running to The Coastal Drip for the iced coffees they'd drink on the way to the airport. He was going to take a few minutes to say goodbye to Meridian before Linda returned.

In the building's lobby, he took a glance around, savoring the memories of the last two weeks. It had been so much more than he'd hoped for, and he hated having to leave, but work beckoned, and he was ready to get back to it.

Meridian didn't work on Saturdays, but she'd told Mason she would be in the lobby, and that's where he found her, in the bright green club chair, reading a book.

"Time to go, Meri!" he called, dragging his rolling bags towards the door. He dropped his backpack next to them and moved across the room to give Meri a hug.

"Take care of yourself. Send a postcard. Keep living right," she said as she stepped into his arms.

"You do the same, please. I hope to be back for July Fourth. Dad's planning a family visit."

Meri patted him on the back before letting him go. "Sounds good. Maybe Linda will be back then, too..."

Mason knew she was fishing for information. "I hope so. We'll see."

She furrowed her brows and glanced outside. "She will be busy, though. Hard to get away when you run your own business."

Odd. Linda hadn't had any trouble getting away for the last three weeks. What would prevent her from coming in July?

"She seems to have no trouble traveling while she works," he responded.

"Right. Right. But if she opens her own store, it will be harder." Meri shrugged her shoulders. "But I hope to see you both back this summer."

"Right." Mason wasn't sure what was right or what he was agreeing with. It seemed Meri knew something he didn't. That hurt. Why would Linda confide in Meri and not him?

A car horn sounded, and they glanced towards the door. Linda gave a wave, and Mason waved back, making his way towards his bags, Meri a few paces behind him.

"Have a safe flight," Meri called as Mason opened the door.

"Thanks! See you!" he shouted as the door closed behind him.

Linda popped the trunk, and Mason tossed in his bags. He checked his watch. There was plenty of time to make his flight.

In the cool car, Linda pointed to one of the drinks in the cup holders. "That one's yours."

"Thanks." He lifted it and twirled it, watching the ice cubes mix the cream around. "And thank you for driving me."

"Not a problem."

Silence fell, and Mason thought about what Meri had said. Was Linda considering opening her own store? That was a big jump from selling notepads and journals. He thought about the commitment of owning a retail location. The hours, the lack of holidays and days off. His leg shook, and he glanced at the cup.

"One espresso shot or two?" he asked.

"One." Linda gave him a quick glance and changed lanes. They'd be at the airport before he knew it, and he wanted to savor this time with her. He pushed aside the nagging fear that life would move them in different directions before they had a chance to make it work.

He shifted in his seat to watch her. Her pink hair was in a high ponytail, making the unicorn-sitting-on-a-pool-float earrings more noticeable. She said she was going to spend the rest of the day poolside, and he noticed the bathing-suit tie lying on the back of her T-shirt. Glancing into the back seat, he saw her large stuffed tote bag. She probably didn't even need to go back to the condo; she could go right to the pool when she got back.

"What time will you be home tomorrow?" he asked.

"About 7 p.m. if all goes right. I'll have to get my cats from Laurel and then drive home. Sorcha said she's making dinner, which I think means she's ordering Chinese takeout. I'll miss the sun and the water, but I'm ready to sleep in my own bed."

She laughed, and her sunglasses slipped down her nose. He smiled as he watched her scrunch her nose to get them back in place.

"Funny. I never thought about that. Not sure what *my* bed would feel like. They're always temporary."

"Oh, I love my pillow-top mattress. I sleep so well in it. Took me a week to adjust to the bed in the condo."

"Pillow-top, huh? Sounds heavenly."

He was making small talk, but he wanted to say so much more. He wanted to tell her he was going to miss her every day until he could see her again. And he wanted to tell her he'd buy her a plane ticket to come see him anytime. If she had flexibility to work in Florida, then she could work in Seattle, and she had said she wanted to visit Seattle. It's why he'd picked that city.

But the drive to the airport was not the time to confess these things. It would feel like setting a broken bone, then immediately removing the cast, saying "Just kidding", and removing any sort of stability when it was needed most.

He would wait and see how things progressed when they were apart. He planned to communicate every day, even if it was only a quick text message. They needed to stay in touch. They needed to maintain a sense of normalcy and day-to-day interaction.

Then he needed to find a way for them to be together, permanently.

Déjà vu, Linda thought, pulling into the airport, watching the signs for Mason's terminal. He was taking the same airline Sorcha had flown two weeks ago.

Pulling to the curb, she flicked on her hazard lights and checked the mirror before jumping out. Mason had already popped the trunk and was shrugging into his backpack.

She grabbed the smaller of the two roller bags and put it on the ground, glancing behind her at the car pulling up. She hated having to hurry. Maybe she should have parked and walked him to the terminal.

"Got everything?" she asked.

Mason pulled the handles up on both roller bags, then turned his focus on her. He held out his arms, and she stepped into them, resting her head on his chest.

Tears stung her eyes. *Don't cry!*

Mason hugged her tightly and rocked gently.

"Got to keep it moving!" yelled a security guard walking on the sidewalk.

Mason sighed and pulled back slightly. "I hate good-byes."

"Then don't say it."

"See you later, then?"

"That works."

He let go of her and put his hands on her cheeks. He leaned in for a kiss, and the noise and motion of the airport drop-off lane melted away. Linda sighed as her lips found their place on his.

As much delight as she felt from his kiss, it was gone too soon. He pulled back, smiled, and quickly kissed her nose.

"I'll call or text when I get in."

"Do that."

He stepped back and grabbed the handles of the suitcases. As he walked away, she watched him get swallowed up by the automatic doors, and her body shuddered.

"You owe me four hundred dollars for the veil," Laurel stated as soon as she opened the door to her apartment.

Linda, standing on the welcome mat, felt all the enjoyment from her time in Florida get sucked out of her.

"Hello to you, too," she said, stepping into the apartment. "I don't have that much cash on me. Can I mobile pay you?"

"No rush. Just wanted to remind you." Laurel's voice rose and fell like she was speaking to one of the six-year-olds in her classroom.

Buddy ambled out of the bedroom and circled Linda's leg. She reached down and scooped the cat into her arms, giving him kisses and coos. He purred in her ear. "Fine. I'll send it when I get home." Linda would send her a check and hope the snail mail would do its thing.

"Or maybe we can go shopping together to replace it. That would be fun!"

Linda wasn't sure about making that promise but murmured something that sounded like agreement.

"Other than the veil incident, the cats seemed to have a good time." Laurel walked towards her kitchen. "Want a drink?"

"Nope. I want to get the cats and get home. Sorcha's making dinner."

"Oh. I'd hoped to talk to you about the plans for the bridal shower. You know. Make sure everything is on track. Erin said—"

"It's on track."

"I didn't finish."

"It's on track, Laurel. Can we talk tomorrow? It was a rough flight. Turbulence. And I was stuck between a man who promptly fell asleep, drooled, and snored the whole way, and a woman who was knitting. Which sounds harmless, but her elbow knocked my arm every five seconds. It was torture."

"Testy. Fine. Call me tomorrow. I want to make sure—"

"I know you do. I promise it will be fantastic. It's under control."

Laurel's bridal shower seemed to be the only thing Linda had under control at the moment. Her heart was freaking out, wondering why she hadn't changed the destination of her flight to Seattle, and her brain was calculating and planning and imagining everything that might be needed to expand her side hustle.

She needed to get home and gain perspective on everything. Time back in her own home, in her normal routine, would give her that.

The vacation bubble—beach vibes, blueberry treats, and floating in the pool—popped. She was back to reality.

Chapter 20

While her twin greeted her with demands and attitude, Sorcha greeted her like a long-lost bestie. Just what she needed.

Entering their apartment, Linda's eyes swept over everything in her line of sight: their living room, dining room, and kitchen. It was a modest apartment where she'd lived some of the best times of her life.

She'd lived with Sorcha for four years and often wondered which one of them would move on first. Her money was on Sorcha falling in love and moving out. She had plans to convert Sorcha's bedroom into a craft room/office, and now maybe her business command center, when Sorcha left.

Sorcha squeezed her twice and grabbed one of the cat carriers out of her hand. "Oh, the babies are home!" she squealed, quickly putting the carrier down and releasing the latch. Missy ran out quickly and ran to the empty food dish. She sat primly and thumped her tail twice.

"Patience," Linda called, opening the door to Buddy's carrier. He followed his sister and meowed.

"Feed me, meow!" Sorcha called, making "meow" sound like "now".

Linda dropped the carry-on bag and rolled her shoulders. "I'm glad to be home. What's for dinner?"

"Takeout."

"Chinese?"

"Yeppers."

"Yum. I'll run out and grab my suitcases. Will you please feed the little monsters?"

Thirty minutes later, Linda and Sorcha were sitting at the small round table in their dining space. The girls had painted the dinette a bright, sunny yellow. They'd found the set sitting in an alley on garbage day. They'd looked at each other, yelled "Score!" and grabbed it.

"Now, tell me how the rest of the time went with hottie, Mason," Sorcha said, dipping an egg roll in ketchup.

Linda always wanted to eye roll at Sorcha's preferred way of eating an egg roll, but she refrained. It was losing its strangeness, now that she'd seen her roommate do it a hundred times. "It was good. We patched things up. Found our friendship again."

"Only friendship?"

"For now. To be real, I think I could fall back in love with him, if I haven't already. But the long-distance thing...it's so hard. We've reconnected, but you can't build the trust needed for a relationship in just two weeks."

"Says you." Sorcha scooped another spoonful of fried rice onto her plate.

Linda sighed. "He hurt me deeply before. And he loves what he does. He loves nursing. He loves moving somewhere new every few months. How can I compete with that?"

"It's not a competition when it's love." Sorcha shook her head, her eyes dancing with conviction. "You figure it out and make it work. Where's he off to now?"

"Seattle."

"Hey, you said you would like to go there!"

"I know. I told him that, too. Might be why he picked it. He was debating going there or Portland, Maine. He chose Seattle."

"See? He's got it bad for you if he's picking where he'll live based on your suggestion."

"I didn't suggest it. I just said I wanted to see the city."

"You should go. When can you go?"

Linda laughed. "I think I'll wait until I'm invited first. We'll see how things go once he gets settled and I get back to normalcy."

"Normalcy is for muggles, Lulu."

Linda thought about sharing her new business ideas with Sorcha. Sorcha was always her biggest cheerleader. But as with Mason, she worried that sharing something too soon could ruin it. Take away her drive for it. Better to keep those ideas to herself for now. If things went her way, she might share something cool soon.

By Tuesday night, Mason was bored. In the prior seventy-two hours, he'd unpacked, studied the transportation routes, worked three shifts at the new hospital, stocked up on groceries, lifted weights in the apartment building's gym twice, and picked up his phone fifty times to call Linda.

He'd only texted twice.

Once on Sunday night to make sure she was home (she was), and again on Monday night to see how her workday went (she said it was fine).

He'd had a grueling shift. A morning commuter bus had crashed, sending eighteen people into the hospital before seven. By noon, he'd assisted with six of the patients. He disliked working in the emergency department. Patients were scared, in awful shape, and wanted to be anywhere but there.

Being the new guy didn't give him a lot of choice on rotations. He went wherever the hospital had the greatest need.

That was another reason to consider a permanent gig. He could get into a line of work he excelled at. He could master the skills needed for advancement. Perhaps he could even supervise or teach.

He'd dreamed of that at one point. Being highly skilled. That's when he'd planned to be a pediatric orthopedist, a doctor like his dad and sister. Before his mom got sick.

Back then he was driven, secretly competing with his older sister for dad's admiration and attention.

All that changed with his mom's diagnosis. He saw the days for what they were—a gift, fragile, not guaranteed.

He'd shifted focus from long-term goals to short-term gains. How could he help people as soon as possible? Spend time with his mom and not countless hours studying? How could he...

Glancing at the clock that came with the furnished apartment, he waited. It was only 4 p.m. in Illinois. He'd wait until after five to call Linda. Even though her workday was flexible, he wanted her full attention. He didn't want her to be working on an email or chatting with her boss when he called.

His eyes swept the apartment. It had looked better in pictures than it did in real life. Typical. The trendy gray walls had looked cool and interesting. Now they looked cold and impersonal.

The framed black and white photographs of the Space Needle, the Pop Culture Museum, and the Pacific Science Center seemed lifeless and boring.

He knew his malaise came from missing Linda. Usually a new city, a new job, and new digs energized him, made him want to fill his Instagram feed with photos of the interesting places and sights. Now he wanted to fill his feed with pictures of a certain gorgeous, pink-haired woman.

He needed to get out and get some air. Rain or no rain. An hour's walk around the neighborhood would clear his head, maybe even provide inspiration for an Insta-pic.

Chapter 21

On Saturday morning, Linda walked into the coffee shop and marched to the counter. She ordered an extra-large hazelnut latte with an extra shot of espresso. She was going to be productive this morning, and the caffeine would help.

Finding an open table in the courtyard, she settled in and pulled out her tablet. She had a list of tasks to complete and wanted to prioritize them before getting started.

She'd been working for an hour when a shadow fell over the table. She looked up to find Wyatt standing beside her.

"Hey," he said, his deep blue eyes captivating her gaze.

"Oh, hi! How are you?"

"Good. Better now that you're here." He swished the towel in his hand back and forth.

Sorcha was right; he was definitely flirting.

"Florida was great, but it's good to be home."

"The tan looks great on you."

Her cheeks flushed. "Thanks. I miss the beach already."

He looked over his shoulder. "Customers. I better get back to work. See you around."

"See you."

Well, that wasn't completely telling. Sort of flirting. Sort of being friendly. Excellent customer service.

Oh, well. She wasn't here for Wyatt. She was here to get work done, and she had. Standing, she stretched and took her coffee tumbler back to the counter for a refill of regular coffee.

Back at her table, she pulled out a sketch pad and a brand-new set of colored pencils she'd bought the day before. It was time to play.

Mason spent his Saturday morning exploring the city and getting groceries. Having his first Saturday off in Seattle surprised him, but he needed to be at the hospital bright and early on Sunday morning, so he took advantage of the time.

Sightseeing kept him occupied enough until he could call Linda. The two-hour time difference was annoying. Maybe his next rotation would be in the Central Time Zone. Lots of options and plenty of unknown places to discover.

Once his groceries were put away, he grabbed a glass of water and went to the tiny balcony overlooking a baseball field. There was enough room for a small round table and two stools on the balcony. Big enough.

He took a picture of the view and sent it to Linda with "Can you talk?" attached.

She replied with a quick yes, so he called.

"Hi, you. Great view," she said. He smiled at the sound of her voice. It'd been a week. Seven long days without it.

"Hi, yourself. Yeah, it's a good one. Pretty cool city. Can't wait for you to visit."

Linda chuckled. "That didn't take long. Are you settled in?"

"Yes. Lots of great people at the hospital. A few friend-lies in the building. I've figured out the transit system. The apartment is a little farther away than I typically like, but it's all good. Working it out. How are you? How was your week back at home?"

He couldn't wait to hear every detail she would share. It still bothered him that Meri had mentioned a retail situation. He hoped Meri had confused Linda with someone else.

"It was good. I miss Seaside Bay, but it was good to see my kitties and Sorcha. And to sleep in my bed."

"The pillow-top for the princess, right?"

"I'm no princess," she protested.

"Think again, Sunshine."

Whoa. He hadn't called her Sunshine since they were ten years old. He'd gotten a black eye the last time he had.

"Sunshine? Really?" She laughed, the sound like warm honey.

"Yikes. That slipped out. I remember what happened last time. I take it back. What are you doing this morning?"

He pictured her in her pajamas on the couch, a book and coffee within reach.

"I'm hanging out at our favorite coffee shop. I did some work, and now I'm doodling."

"You're drawing?"

"I said doodling. Playing around."

"I see. What are your plans for the rest of the day?"

Gosh, was this conversation boring? Was he boring her?

"I'm meeting up with your sister to plan some last-minute things for Laurel's shower."

"Sorry."

"I said—"

He cut her off with a laugh.

"Oh," she said. "Erin. Ha, ha. She's wonderful to me. I don't know what your problem is."

"I could say the same thing about your sister. Well, don't let Erin bulldoze you into doing too much. She should do her fair share."

"I'm sure she will. Hold on."

Mason could hear a man's voice talking to Linda. It sounded as though she'd pulled her phone away from her face, but she hadn't muted him. Who was she talking to? Was she meeting with her boss on a Saturday?

"Sorry. I'm back."

"Who was that?"

"Wyatt. He works here."

Wyatt. Not the "barista" or the "coffee dude" or "guy who works here", Wyatt. She said favorite coffee shop, so a place she frequented. He couldn't let that get under his skin.

"Well. Tell Erin hello from me when you see her. I work a seven-to-seven shift tomorrow. Can I call you tomorrow night?"

"Yes, that'd be great. See you."

She hung up too fast. Was Wyatt hovering nearby, waiting for her to get off the phone? He put the phone down and looked at the view. Past the ball diamond was a large park, and beyond that, he could see Puget Sound. Sunlight hit the water, sparkling like a dance. It was pretty, but not as pretty as the view from the condo in Seaside Bay. And not nearly as pretty as Linda.

Chapter 22

"So, all systems go for the bridal shower?" Mason asked.

It was three weeks later, the day before Laurel's shower. They'd talked on the phone frequently, texted every day, and Linda was getting accustomed to this new normal.

It was fun knowing she'd hear from Mason each day. Sometimes it was six in the morning, before she'd even woken, sometimes it was mid-afternoon, as she was trying to wrap up work for Grady before she started on product development for her new line of business in the evening, or it could even be late evening if Mason had worked second-shift hours.

She'd received some sample packages from various printers and was comparing quality and price for her first order of to-do lists with magnets on the back for refrigerators. After selecting her favorite designs, she hoped to have the first order in hand within two weeks. She'd talked to Polly in Tampa, and Polly had promised to place an order as soon as Linda was ready.

Talking to Mason frequently helped, but it wasn't as good as seeing him in person. There was no chance to rest her head on his shoulder, or clasp his hand, or stare into his confident brown eyes.

"We're ready. It should be a beautiful event. I hope Laurel loves it."

"She'd better. I know you worked hard on it."

He was right, she had. From designing the invitation to selecting the venue to planning the menu, she wanted Laurel's shower to be perfect. Yes, Erin helped, but she left the major decisions up to Linda, saying Linda knew her sister best.

Which she did. As much as she was looking forward to having the shower behind her, she was looking forward to spending the day with her family and Laurel's closest friends. Two of their aunts had flown in from New York to attend, and her mother was over the moon. Her first daughter was getting married, and she was already dreaming about her future grandchildren.

"Thanks for that." Linda looked at the clock. She needed to leave in twenty minutes to go to her nail appointment. Laurel would rail at the current state of her broken, chipped fingernails. "What are your plans for the day?"

"Going for a jog, then I'm going to contact my placement manager about my next gig."

"Your next gig? Aren't you in Seattle for two more months?"

"I am. But if I wait until the last minute, I won't have a lot of choice about where I get to go next. I want to tell him now that I want to be placed in the same time zone as you. It will make keeping in touch a lot easier. I'm always calculating what time it is for you whenever I look at my watch. Which I do frequently."

Wow. His next place? Linda was hoping he was going to look for some place closer. Chicago, Peoria, or even better, Bloomington. The Central Time Zone could land him in south Texas or northwestern North Dakota. Too far away!

"Oh," she managed.

"Speaking of Seattle, when are you coming to see me?"

"Things are so crazy with Laurel's wedding coming up. I don't know."

"Come on. Take a break and come see me. I'll buy the plane ticket. What about June seventh? Come for the weekend. You'll love the Space Needle and Pikes Peak. I can't wait to show you around."

"What's Pikes Peak?"

"Sorry, I mean Pike Place. The fish market. They throw fish."

"That does not sound appetizing. Let me check my schedule and get back to you."

She had orders coming that would need to be shipped out. And she had a list of local stores to visit to see if they would carry her stuff.

"You do that and get back to me. Have fun at the shower. Can't wait to hear how it goes!"

Really, Mason? "I'll update you, stat."

He laughed, the sound filling her insides with a warm glow. She missed him and knew she'd make the time to go to Seattle. She hung up and added "check for flights" to her growing to-do list.

The shower guests had left; only Laurel, their mother Nicole, Erin, and Linda remained. They were sitting around the table, relaxing and gathering the willpower to haul all the gifts to the cars. They'd need more than just Laurel's car to get it all to her house. Much to Linda's relief, Erin volunteered to be the second pack mule.

"If the wedding goes half as well as today, it will be perfect!" Laurel declared. Linda glanced at her sister's wineglass and wondered how many she'd had.

"It will be perfect!" Nicole said. "I have no doubts. Three cheers to Linda and Erin for making this day beautiful. From the food to the decorations, you did a fantastic job."

"Thanks!" Linda held up her glass in response to her mother's words. It'd been perfect. They hadn't missed a single detail. Now most of the pressure was off her. All eyes would be on Laurel. It was her big day. Linda just needed to show up, not trip walking down the aisle, and dye her hair.

Darn. She'd forgotten about that part.

She didn't want to dye her hair. The colors were part of who she was. She wouldn't stop. She swirled the wine in her glass, contemplating. Finally, she had it. She'd get a wig. There were wigs that looked natural. Heck, it would probably be even faster getting ready for the wedding. She would throw her hair in a net and set the wig on her head. She pulled her phone out of her pocket discreetly, and added "look for wig" to her list.

"Mom, can you help me re-pin my hair?" Laurel asked. "I know a few curls fell out when I was hugging everyone goodbye."

Their mother nodded, and they left for the restroom. Erin leaned back in her chair and looked at Linda. "So, Mason said you two met up in Florida."

"Well, we were both there at the same time. We didn't intentionally meet up."

"Have you talked since?"

"A few times."

"I knew it. He can't hide anything from me."

"It's been nice to reconnect."

Erin probably didn't know how much it had hurt Linda when he'd left, unless Laurel had told her.

"That's good. I wish he'd grow up and stop moving around so much. He's twenty-eight, time to act like an adult. But he won't. He'll never come back to central Illinois, anyway. Too many memories of Mom. He can't handle it."

Linda hummed noncommittally.

"Dad and Terry think he may end up in Seaside Bay. The best memories were at the beach. Mom got sick here and never made it back there."

"Uh, huh," Linda mumbled. She wished her mom and Laurel would return. Looking down at her arms, she scratched at a small rash on her wrist. Hives. Erin's questioning about her status with Mason was making her nervous.

"Anyway, what do I know? Mason has surprised me more than a few times." Erin gave a shrug of her shoulders, the smile not reaching her eyes.

Linda reached over and squeezed Erin's hand. She didn't know why, but Erin needed it. Linda knew Mason's grief; she'd seen it up close. Erin's grief was different, but it was still there. It always would be. How could you ever get over losing your mother?

Erin squeezed Linda's hand like she was grasping a life preserver.

Was Erin right? Would Mason ever stop moving around? She'd never be able to establish a retail store if she attached her heart to Mason. He loved to travel and explore. She couldn't manage a retail store with that lifestyle, not unless it was on wheels.

Chapter 23

Mason's phone rang, pulling him away from submitting the Etsy order of three task organizers from Linda's store. He wasn't sure he'd use them, but he wanted to support her business. He stared at the offending noisemaker in disbelief. Erin was calling.

"What's up?" he asked, hoping no one was ill.

"Hey. I was talking to Terry, and she said she thought you were going to stay with them when you're home for Laurel's wedding. I said I thought you were staying with me. Just wanted to confirm."

"Oh." This was easy. "I'll stay wherever it's most convenient for you guys."

"Geez. Make a dang decision, will ya? We don't care."

"Fine. I'll stay with Dad and Terry."

"That wasn't so hard, now, was it? Hey, I chatted with Linda at Laurel's bridal shower on Saturday. She said you guys reconnected in Florida."

"She did?" That didn't seem like Linda. He would have guessed she'd be more discreet.

"Well, connected, at least. Honestly, Dad already told me. So, what happened?"

Mason considered how much he would share. Erin could be an ally in this thing, or she could be a pain in the keister. "It surprised me to see her there. But we got caught up, volunteered for Meridian, hung out. Not much to report."

"So, you patched things up. Romantically?"

Mason relived the most romantic moments with Linda during those two weeks in Florida. The way he'd caught her in his arms at the festival and kissed her. Falling asleep, holding her on the couch. The kiss goodbye at the airport. There were moments, but not enough of them. "No, just friendly. I'm trying to talk her into visiting me. We'll see where it goes. I asked her to be my date for Laurel's wedding, but she turned me down."

"Rightfully so. You broke her heart. There's no way she'd get back with you. You weren't here, you didn't see how bad it was."

"And you did? Didn't realize you and Linda were so close."

"Well, I heard about it from Laurel."

"And she doesn't exaggerate?"

"Maybe. Sometimes. But not about this. Linda deserves better. Let her go."

"I don't know that I can do that, Erin. Is there anything else you need today? I have a shift starting soon."

"No. That's all, Nurse Mason."

She loved that dig.

He hung up the phone and groaned. He wanted to vent to Linda, but he couldn't talk to her about that conversation.

He texted her instead.

Mason: Did you book your flight yet?

Linda: Great minds. I did that just now.

Mason: Yeah? Sweet! When?

Linda: June 8th. Quick trip. Need to return on the 10th. Will email the itinerary.

Mason opened the calendar app on his phone and marked the days Linda would visit. Only forty-eight hours; he had some planning to do.

The retail clerk handed Linda's credit card back to her. "Here you go," the too-perky young lady with the too-perky curls said, in a too-perky voice.

Linda wasn't sure what annoyed her more, the clerk's voice or the fact that she'd paid three hundred and ninety dollars to replace her sister's wedding veil. She hoped that the beautiful cathedral-length veil with hand-embroidered floral detail would make it through Laurel's wedding with no further incidents. Linda was going to lay claim to it the day after Laurel's wedding. Not that it was her style, but by golly, she was not paying for another veil in her lifetime.

Beside her, Laurel sighed. "Only four weeks to go, and now I can say I'm ready. Thank you for replacing my veil, Lindy."

"You're welcome." Linda thought about Buddy and Missy. She was going to withhold their favorite cat treats for the next month. Well, she probably would.

The clerk handed the carefully wrapped and protected veil to Laurel as Linda tucked her credit card back in her wallet.

The little piece of plastic was getting a lot of use. Besides replacing Laurel's veil, she had all the other expenses of being in a wedding party—her maid of honor dress, her shoes, a hotel room, gifts, and hosting the bridal shower.

Plus a flight to Seattle to see Mason in two weeks.

And she'd placed product sample orders with four different producers to compare quality this week, as well.

Focus on the gains, not the losses. New brother-in-law, time with Mason, and products she could show to local retail stores.

Laurel made a show of carefully draping the packaged veil over her arm. "Do you have time for lunch, or do you need to rush back home?"

"I can eat." *Not sure I can afford to.*

"Great. There's a new restaurant near the university that I've been wanting to try."

Thirty minutes later, they sat and sipped soft drinks, waiting for their food. Laurel had chatted nonstop about wedding plans and outstanding tasks ever since they'd left the bridal shop.

Linda chimed in as needed and kept imagining a new printable that she could create, a bridal countdown checklist to track all the last-minute things to do. Laurel's mind seemed filled to nearly bursting with minutiae.

"So," Laurel said, "have you found a date for the wedding?"

Found a date, like they were standing around waiting to be chosen. This wasn't an eighth-grade dance. "No...but I was thinking about asking Mason."

Laurel's perfectly manicured eyebrows rose up, then down. "Really?"

Now that it was out there, no taking it back. "Yeah. He asked me when we were in Florida. I said no. Thought it would be too weird. But we've been talking or texting daily, and I'm going to go to Seattle to visit him. If that goes well, I'll ask him then."

"When are you going? There's lots of wedding prep to do."

"In two weeks." The server put their salad plates in front of them. "It'll be a quick visit. I fly out on Friday night and come home on Sunday. There's nothing scheduled for your wedding that weekend. It's the only weekend we don't have something planned. Only time I could go."

Picking up a fork, Laurel nodded. "I see. So, you might get back together with him?"

"Please don't share this with Erin yet. I don't want the two of you getting involved. I'm not sure it will work, but it was good to reconnect. Good to get past the hurt and anger."

"Are you sure you're past it?"

Linda considered, chewing slowly. "Yes. We talked, and he explained where his head was then. I get it. We're both more mature now. Maybe things could be different."

"We can hope." Laurel sounded unconvinced.

Chapter 24

"And then we can go to the Pop Culture Museum. After that, we'll go to the Rubber Chicken Museum and then—"

"Whoa. Hold up. Did you say Rubber Chicken?" Linda asked. Did Mason think she wasn't paying attention to him and throwing random words into sentences?

After several text messages, Mason had found her at the airport and now they were taking a rideshare back to his apartment.

She was looking out the window at the buildings and street signs flying by. The unfortunate thing about getting in so late was not being able to see the things that made Seattle unique. She'd be in Seattle for less than forty-eight hours, and she wanted to become familiar with the city, not spend all their time in museums.

"Yes." Mason's enthusiasm was contagious, even about chickens. "Rubber Chicken Museum. Sounds bonkers, doesn't it? I think we have to check it out."

Since she couldn't see much out the window anyway, she shifted around to look at him. "I was hoping to see the sights, not museum-hop."

"Oh, sure. Not a problem. Whatever you want to do. I haven't done much sightseeing myself, as I was waiting for your visit. There are several brochures in my apartment. You can look over them in the morning and we'll go from there. We have options. Harbor cruise, walk around, or there's a bus tour. Whatever." He paused and looked sheepish. "I'm so sorry. I'm excited and rambling on and on. Didn't mean to make plans for you. I want to do whatever *you* want to do. If you want to hang out in my apartment and watch TV, that's fine. I'm just happy and thankful that you came." He took her hand, giving it a squeeze.

The warmth of his hand calmed her nerves. On the flight, she'd worried about how the weekend would pan out. Would they get along in a new environment? It had been easy to reconnect with him in Seaside Bay, where they had so many happy memories together. Would that translate to a new city? And with Laurel's wedding looming, would she have the courage to ask Mason to be her date?

Linda could barely keep her eyes open, and they were still waiting for their main course. They'd walked for miles, seen many of the famous attractions in downtown Seattle and were now eating dinner at nine o'clock on Saturday night. Jet lag was kicking her butt.

"Wow. What a day," Mason said, leaning forward, his forearms resting on the table.

"I can't believe we made it to so many places today, but I still wish I had more time to explore. Can't believe I have to go home tomorrow. I just got here!" Linda lamented, taking a long drink of her diet soda.

"I know, but you can come back." Mason raised his shoulders. "Anytime."

"Yeah, right. It's not the cheapest flight. Plus, with Laurel's wedding and my new venture, I won't have time before you leave for your next location." Linda dropped her gaze to her fork, which she straightened. She hated the thought of him moving on; she was certain it wouldn't be to Bloomington. It would be to another town she'd have to visit.

"About that." Mason took a deep breath.

"What?" Linda braced for the worst.

"I may have an opportunity to stay here. The head nurse in geriatrics is impressed with my work ethic, and she's talked to me about taking on a permanent position. It would be a good position with a salary bump. And it would give me the chance to own my own espresso machine." He smiled, and Linda was reminded of the wonderful coffees he'd made for her in Florida with the machine he'd convinced his dad to buy for their condo.

Linda sat stunned. He was considering something permanent? In Seattle?

"Geriatrics? You haven't mentioned that as a particular interest of yours."

"No, but I think it would be a good fit for me." He looked down at his hands as he pulled back further into his seat. She knew he meant to hide it from her, but she could see the flash of pain in his eyes. "I can't handle losing another kid."

Her heart squeezed. She could not imagine the horror of dealing with that. "I see. But Seattle...isn't this the first time you've been here? You said yourself you haven't done a lot of sightseeing yet. Why would you settle here?"

The words tasted like milk that had curdled. She shivered.

"True, but I've gotten around my neighborhood and the area around the hospital. They're great."

He looked at her again, and she tried to smile at him. They were friends. She would support him. They'd been in the friend zone most of their lives. It was precious, and she wouldn't lose it again.

"That's wonderful. I bet your dad is proud of you."

"Oh, I haven't talked to him about it yet. I will. What do you think of Seattle? Could you see yourself moving here?"

Moving here?! Away from her family and friends? She could, but did she want to?

"I've been in this city for twenty-four hours, and yes, it's great, but I wouldn't make such a decision about where to live based on a one-day visit. I'm not...adventurous like you. My life is comfortable. I know the baristas at my favorite coffee shop. There's a place in Miller Park where I love to sit and read a good book. I go to dinner at my parents' at least twice a month. Besides, I want to expand my side business, and maybe make it my entire business."

"You'd leave Grady?"

"Wow. You make it sound like we're together." She laughed uncomfortably. "I work for Grady, but more importantly, he's a friend. I would still have his friendship if I didn't work for him. Sure, he wouldn't be that jazzed about losing me. I'm pretty amazing, you know," she said, trying to lighten the tone of the conversation.

Mason chuckled. "I know."

She continued, "Grady would be happy to see me develop a business. He's told me many times the only thing holding me back is me. I'm trying to take that to heart."

Mason said he wanted her to chase her dreams, but it was Grady who'd mentored her and given her the confidence that she could be successful in business. He asked her opinions on important decisions for the business, and when he ultimately disagreed or went a different route, he explained which factors had influenced his decision, so she could develop her skills.

The server brought their dinners and asked if they needed anything else. When Linda shook her head no, Mason dismissed the server. Linda picked up a fork and pushed the scallops around.

Mason shifted forward and cut into his steak. "Honestly, I didn't think you would leave your job. You seemed so dedicated to it. And I thought that moving here would be easy for you, because you could continue to work remotely. But if you're going to leave that job, what will you do, exactly?"

Linda took a bite but didn't taste her food. "Create a quirky but functional line of paper products that can be sold in retail stores. To do that well, I need to devote one hundred and ten percent of my attention to it. And..." She dropped her eyes. "Maybe someday I will open my own brick and mortar store. Not right away, but someday."

"A retail store? Wow! That's risky. But cool, definitely cool," he rushed to add.

"See? I'm not in a position to move right now. Maybe someday." She didn't add it would take a heck of a lot more convincing to get her to move out of Illinois.

"I get it. Sure. But that's okay. We can figure it out. Together."

"Aren't you going to eat?" she asked, eying the untouched steak on his plate.

"Yeah."

They each picked at their meal but didn't relish the food.

By the time they left the restaurant, Linda had decided that she wouldn't ask Mason to be her date for Laurel's wedding. She needed to put boundaries around her heart. Brick and mortar boundaries.

Chapter 25

There were only seven days until Laurel's wedding, and Linda's to-do list had seven remaining items: break in shoes, wrap gift, make card, try on dress, get nails done, thrift evening purse, buy wig, and find a date. Not necessarily in that order.

She'd been home from Seattle for almost a week. Mason still texted her every day, but there seemed to be less enthusiasm than before. She wasn't sure if that was coming from Mason or if it was just how she felt about the situation.

She hadn't asked him to be her date for Laurel's wedding. She couldn't. It was never going to work between them, as much as she'd dreamed it would. He said he was ready to settle down. That was wonderful, but Illinois did not seem to be an option for him. She understood that home held many painful memories for him. But this was her home. Her family was here, her favorite pizza place was two blocks away, and she had no desire to uproot and move.

All Mason had done for the last six years was uproot and move. That worked for him. It wouldn't work for her. And she wouldn't ask him to change, not if he loved to move constantly. She'd seen the way his eyes had lit up as they'd made their way around Seattle. There was always something cool and new around every corner. It filled Mason with energy and joy.

A new city was cool but overwhelming to her. She enjoyed the newness while on a vacation, for three days or seven days or slightly longer, but there was the sweet anticipation of the end. At the end of vacation, she could go home, sleep in her own bed and hug her kitties. She couldn't imagine moving with two cats all the time. It would be too disruptive for them.

She sighed, looking at the to-do list. Most were simple, easy to accomplish, they just needed some dedicated time. But finding a date...she hated asking a guy out. Sure, she was capable. She'd done it once, and it had worked fairly well. They'd made it to date number three before they'd both decided that was enough to know there was no spark.

Sorcha's suggestion about Wyatt came back to her. He was friendly and flirty. It was a lot to ask—the wedding was in one week—but there was a chance he'd say yes, and she was going for it.

Linda walked into the Up 'Til Dawn coffee shop and glanced around. Wyatt typically worked Saturdays, but it wasn't a guarantee. She stepped to the counter and placed her order with "Jill", according to the barista's name tag.

She asked Jill if Wyatt was working and the girl said yes, that he was grabbing some supplies from the stockroom and would be out soon.

Linda took a seat and waited. When Wyatt strolled out of the stockroom, she smiled and gave him a little wave.

Wyatt held a stack of boxes so he couldn't wave. He nodded towards her and gave her a goofy grin.

He was tall and lanky with black hair that could use a trim and no facial hair. Linda wondered if he had ever played basketball or been teased about his height. Something to ask him about, perhaps on a date. Probably not at her sister's wedding, though.

Wyatt placed the boxes on the counter, said a few words to Jill, and came around to say hello to Linda.

"Hi, there," Linda said as he approached.

"Hey. How's it going? Missed you last weekend."

Linda glanced at the growing line of customers and wondered if Jill was annoyed that Wyatt wasn't helping her. "I was out of town. Seattle."

"Oh yeah, Seattle's cool. Home of grunge."

"Yeah, they say. Umm..." *How to begin?* "I was wondering. I know this is a lot to ask, and I fully expect you to say no."

Wyatt's eyebrows rose, but he grinned.

"My sister is getting married next Saturday, and I wondered if you would be my date?" She didn't give him time to answer before plowing forward. "It's local. There will be good food, dancing, and an open bar. You know—"

"Yeah, a wedding. I know." He laughed. "Totally game. I've been meaning to ask you out. You beat me."

"Really?" *Sorcha was right!*

"Yes, was trying to find the best way to bring it up. And you're usually with your friend."

"My roommate, Sorcha."

"Yes. Her. I'm in. Give me your number, and we'll work out the details. I better get back to it. Jilly Bean is backed up." He handed her his phone.

Linda smiled as she punched in her number.

Wyatt took the phone and winked at her. "Text you later," he said, before turning and joining his partner behind the counter.

Linda scratched her wrist and let out a long breath. That was done. There was a certain relief in getting it over with, but a tiny bit of her felt guilty. She knew Mason wasn't bringing a date, and he probably expected to hang out with her at the reception, but now she'd have a buffer.

Wyatt wasn't brick and mortar, but he'd help protect her heart, albeit unwittingly.

Chapter 26

Mason's feet hit the sidewalk like he was running with concrete blocks strapped to them; each stride was a heavy blow that he felt from his toes to his scalp.

The run wasn't giving him any feel-good endorphins today. Or if it was, his crowded thoughts, filled with images of the patient they'd lost today, were squashing all sparks that would make him feel better.

"A job hazard," Mason reminded himself, through clenched teeth. "You knew this when you got into nursing. Heck, you've known this since you were a little kid, and Dad told you his stories about being a doctor."

The pavement continued to punish his body but he kept moving, hoping the sweat and the distance would ease his emotional pain.

Two miles later, he slowed at the edge of a city park. He made his way to the closest bench and sat with a thud.

Breathing deeply, he leaned over and rested his elbows on his knees, watching a line of ants marching between his feet.

He closed his eyes and replayed the last conversation he'd had with Franklin. The thirty-year-old man lamented that he'd put off asking his girlfriend to marry him until he made partner in his law firm. He'd thought by then he would have "made it" in his career and could work on creating the family he'd envisioned.

But a nasty car accident, then sepsis, had taken his life. He'd fought hard. He desperately wanted to live, for all the things he'd put off.

Mason couldn't shake the feeling that God was sending him a direct message with this experience.

"I'm listening," he said, though no one was nearby.

There are no guarantees any of us will get one more day, let alone a lifetime.

Leaning back on the park bench, he looked up and saw the Space Needle. He'd taken Linda there, and while they milled around in the observation deck, he'd had the fleeting thought that it would be a cool place to propose. They weren't ready for that now. But someday...

Someday. There it is. That hopeful word.

Linda was the one for him. He'd known it since he was eleven. She was funny and kind and adventurous. Maybe not as adventurous as he, but she loved to try new games, watch new shows, try new things.

He smiled, thinking about her parasailing story. He'd never thought she'd do something as risky as that, but she had. And she loved it.

He loved her.

Ouch.

He needed to show her. He needed to be the man she wanted.

The minister said the prayer before the rehearsal dinner, getting a chuckle when he prayed for everyone, especially the groom, to show up to church on time the next day.

Once he said, "Amen," Erin poked Linda in the ribs with her fingertip. "Mason might stop by after dinner."

"Really?" Linda asked, filled with both excitement and trepidation.

"Yes, he wanted to see you before tomorrow."

"Oh."

Tomorrow. How was she going to tell Mason that she would have a date for Laurel's wedding? She knew that Laurel had assigned Wyatt to the same table as Mason, much to Linda's dismay. Laurel said it was the only logical place, though Linda thought Wyatt would do fine at the table with four sets of grandparents. But Laurel refused to have one table with nine people.

It was Laurel's wedding; Linda could only push so far.

Wyatt and Mason would be at the "dates" table with the wedding-party dates, plus Linda's boss, Grady, and his girlfriend, Nica. Linda would watch that table closely. She'd probably forget everything she'd planned for her speech; good thing she'd put it in a note on her phone.

A server put a Caesar salad in front of her, and Linda used the food as a distraction to avoid further conversation with Erin. She'd deal with Mason if he showed up.

Wyatt would be a fun date. He'd called her a few times during the week, asking innocuous questions—should he wear a tie, what were her parents like, would he mistake her for her twin. That made Linda laugh. "She'll be in the big white dress. You won't mistake us," she promised.

After the rehearsal dinner, Laurel pulled her aside.

"I thought you were going to color your hair," she said in a hushed voice, because their mother was five feet away.

Linda had doubled down on the color at her latest appointment. Her hair was now bright pink with purple tips. Laurel's mouth had fallen open when Linda had walked into the church for rehearsal. Linda couldn't help but laugh at her sister's expression.

"I did!" Linda responded.

"I meant brown! You look like cotton candy!"

"I've been called worse."

"The pictures! It will ruin the pictures."

"Stop right there. Don't have a hissy fit on the eve of your wedding. It's fine. I have a tasteful, pretty wig for tomorrow. It's a light brunette with soft highlights. I'll look 'respectful.'"

Laurel heaved an exaggerated sigh of relief. "Thank goodness. Does it look like real hair?"

"Yes. It wasn't cheap! It will look fine. For tomorrow, we can pretend I'm a brunette. After the reception, I go back to my preferred hair color—pink!"

"Good." Laurel hugged her. "Thank you. The pink and purple are quite striking. I wish I could pull it off."

"We're twins!" Linda shook her head. "Whatever I can pull off, you could pull off."

"In looks, maybe. But I'm hoping to be promoted to principal soon. I couldn't do it."

The groom-to-be, Patrick, interrupted them. He was taking off and wanted to say good night to his bride.

Watching her sister and Patrick walk away together, his arm draped over her shoulders and Laurel looking up at him, her eyes filled with love, Linda felt a small weight lift from her shoulders. The weight that held a little jealousy that her sister was getting married when she didn't even have a boyfriend. She was at peace and truly happy for her sister.

Someday, I'll find that. Someone who makes me a better person, someone who takes me with all my faults and loves me, anyway.

If she could just get through the wedding. Get through seeing Mason and not being with him. She was determined not to let anything spoil her sister's wedding day. She was going to be the best maid of honor she could be for her sister. And if that meant putting her own heart's desires under lock and key, then so be it.

Chapter 27

Mason's eyes swept the reception hall. The seating chart, drawn artfully on a chalkboard, an homage to Laurel's profession, told him he'd be sitting at table nine. Table tents, printed on eye charts, an homage to the groom's profession, showed him where he belonged for the next few hours.

He walked to the bar to get a beverage and made small talk with an older woman who'd sat in the second row on the groom's side, likely Patrick's grandmother. She was bubbly and excited to get her groove on, or so she said.

At table nine, Mason introduced himself to the people around the table. He met Linda's boss, his girlfriend, the dates of several groomsmen and bridesmaids, and Wyatt.

Wyatt.

Linda's date for the evening.

Mason wanted to dislike the guy, but after speaking to him for several minutes, he found they had a few things in common: they both liked to travel, they both loved to listen to nineties grunge, and they both loved to run.

Does Linda find us similar? Mason pondered as they took their seats. He was happy to sit between the fiancée of the best man and Nica, Grady's girlfriend. Grady sat on the other side of her and the three of them chatted throughout dinner. Wyatt was on the other side of the table, sitting between the girlfriend of one groomsman and a friend of Laurel's from grade school.

When Grady left to get drink refills at the bar, Mason asked Nica about her work. Nica told him about a design she'd done for her former boss that looked like a store-front to be used at booths for farmers' markets or vendor fairs.

"Huh. That's interesting. You know Linda is talking about selling at those types of markets."

"Oh, yeah?" Nica asked, her eyes wide.

"Yes. She wants to make journals, to-do lists, stationery stuff. She thought having a booth where she could sell directly to customers would give her insight into what people want. And she wants to get her products into other boutique stores."

"That's fabulous!"

"I agree. I wonder if she could use something like you mentioned. A cool facade for a booth."

"I'd be happy to help. Though," Nica twisted her mouth, thinking. "I wonder...I've seen people remake old school buses or campers into little stores on wheels. If I were ever to open a store—I'm not, I'd prefer to design and build the store, but if I were—I would do something like that."

"Oh, a SOW, Store On Wheels. That would be perfect. She could drive it around to different locations."

Nica nodded. "You know, if she had one and needed a place to leave it when not in use, I'm sure Grady has a commercial property where it could be stored. Linda knows all the locations as well as Grady. She might think of something."

Nica's shoulders shimmied, and her eyes narrowed. "Another idea. That booth I built that looked like a store?"

"Yes."

"That was for my former boss, Anna Lee. She owned a flower shop in Bloomington. It's called 'In Bloom'. She's since retired, but the store is now owned by a friend of mine, Tilly. There's a large parking lot next to the building. Linda could probably set up her trailer there.

She wouldn't need to have the exact same hours as In Bloom, but with some overlapping, it could help attract customers to both businesses. In Bloom doesn't carry a lot of the items you said Linda wants to sell. I don't know. I'm only brainstorming. It's what I do, as Grady and Linda could tell ya."

His mind swirled, thinking about the possibilities. *If she could take her store with her, she could go anywhere.*

"Nica, you're brilliant!"

"Remind Grady of that, will you?"

Grady leaned over, setting a drink in front of Nica. "Remind me of what?"

"Your girlfriend is brilliant!" Mason said.

"Oh, I know that." Grady nodded as he sat back down. He leaned over and kissed the feisty brunette on the cheek.

Wyatt caught the attention of the table at that moment by raising his hand. "Hey, Grady, what do you do again?"

"I manage the Brightside Bank."

"Sweet. I've been trying to get my resumé in there, but wasn't sure how to go about it," Wyatt said. "Any ideas?"

Grady laughed. "Yes, contact me. Here's my card." He pulled his wallet out and handed a card to Wyatt.

"Thank you! Linda said you were the best boss ever."

Grady shook his head but smiled. "I'm lucky she puts up with me."

The conversation moved on to how everyone knew the bride and/or groom, but Mason mostly tuned it out. He kept thinking about the movable store idea. He loved it and thought Linda would, too. It wouldn't be a silver bullet to patch things up. It wouldn't even be a start, but if there was anything Mason could do to help her, he would.

Mason glanced at the wedding party sitting at the head table. He still couldn't believe Linda had dyed her hair to make her sister happy. He loved the individualism she showed with her vibrant hair colors. But he also under-stood that she loved her sister and would do whatever she could to make Laurel happy. Even dimming her own light so her sister could shine on her wedding day.

It wasn't the first time, and it wouldn't be the last. He thought about Linda's wedding day, and wondered what she would ask Laurel to do, and whether Laurel would comply with her requests.

Then he pictured Linda in a pink dress with matching hair. He smiled at the image.

He saw himself waiting near the officiant, watching Linda walking down the aisle toward him. He had a lot to do to win her over and prove to her they were right for each other. But first, he needed to ensure Wyatt was a one date and done deal.

Linda eyed table nine warily. Again. How could Laurel put Mason at the same table as Grady and Wyatt? *This is not going to end well.*

"Everyone!" Laurel shouted at the wedding party. "After cake is served, we'll need to be ready for the wedding-party dance. Don't rush off."

Linda took a sip of champagne. It was almost time to break free of the assigned seats. She'd be able to mingle, check in with table nine—make sure they weren't exchanging crazy stories about her—and have a dance with Wyatt.

Laurel leaned over and whispered in her ear. "That Wyatt is H. O. T. Hot."

"Yeah," Linda replied. He was dreamy, but he wasn't the one who had filled *her* dreams all week. Mason had. He'd probably haunt her dreams for a long time, but it would eventually fade. He'd go back to Seattle, then on to who knows where. She'd remain. *It's the way it was meant to be.*

She'd have fun with Wyatt until that ran its course. She gave it a good chance for four dates, then it would fizzle. Four dates were four dates. Pretty good considering her track record.

"Is it weird seeing Mason again?" Laurel asked.

Linda couldn't believe her sister was asking so many questions on *her* wedding day. Didn't she have more important things to think about? Oh well, it showed she cared.

"No. It's fine. We're friends. I'm glad he's here to celebrate your special day."

She was. It would be strange for him to not be. His parents were here. Erin was sitting on Linda's right. Their families were always together for important occasions. It was natural.

Twenty minutes later, the wedding-party dance was over, and the wedding party was free to mingle. Linda approached table nine with a mix of trepidation and excitement.

Wyatt rose as she approached and placed a chaste kiss on her cheek. "Great job on your speech," he said close to her ear.

His praise warmed her. "I hope everyone at the table treated you well." She glanced quickly at Mason, who was smiling at her and rising.

He was only five feet away and moving closer. She did not want to be standing in a conversation circle with Wyatt and Mason. Wyatt saw Mason approach and turned to include him in their bubble. *Drats!*

"Linda, Mason told me you two are childhood friends." Wyatt put his hand on her lower back, and she froze.

"Yes, we go way back," Linda replied, thankful Mason hadn't told him they'd been a couple. "Back to skinned knees, action figures, and Barbie dolls."

"I hated it when she took my Barbies," Mason quipped.

"Ha! That's cool." Wyatt nodded. "I was trying to picture you as an awkward teen, but Mason said you were nothing of the sort."

"He's being too kind," Linda returned.

Mason shook his head. "I was the awkward one. Being surrounded by three spunky, sweet, and adventurous girls will do that to a guy."

Linda glanced at the table, waving to Grady and Nica. "And you met my boss. I hope you were both well-behaved."

"Yes, ma'am." Wyatt chuckled. "I'm going to send him my resumé. I'd love to get on at the bank."

What? Wyatt asked Grady for a job? I didn't expect that kind of disaster.

"Oh?" Her calm voice masked her internal dismay.

Mason gave her a look that suggested, "You don't know the half of it". This was not good.

Wyatt elaborated, but she wanted him to stop talking. "Yes. Told Grady that I've wanted to get on there. He gave me his card. If I get a job there, this will be the best wedding I've ever been to."

Linda looked at Mason and rolled her eyes, knowing Wyatt couldn't see her face.

The DJ started a slow song, and Mason reached for her hand.

"You don't mind if I dance with my childhood friend, do you, Wyatt?" Mason looked at Wyatt as he squeezed Linda's hand.

"Oh, but it's a slow song," Wyatt protested.

"Right, and I need to catch up on a few things with Linda about the wedding," Mason replied.

Linda knew they had nothing "to catch up on" for Laurel's wedding.

"In that case, sure," Wyatt agreed.

Linda followed Mason to the dance floor, her hand clasped in his. She saw Erin watching from a tall cocktail table near the dance floor, smiling. That was reassuring.

In the middle of the dance floor, Mason finally turned to her and pulled her close.

"Hey," he whispered, his eyes soft and his smile wide.

"Hey," she whispered back. "How was your dinner conversation?"

"Interesting and lively. Nica is a riot."

"She's spunky, that's for sure. She's good for Grady."

"I get that. He's a good guy. I can see why you enjoy working for him."

Linda nodded but she didn't want to talk about work right now.

They swayed slowly and Linda looked at the other couples on the dance floor. Her parents were dancing. Laurel and Patrick were holding each other; Linda wasn't sure if they were dancing or simply hugging, and numerous other swaying couples surrounded them.

The lights had been turned down after dinner, and the dance floor was illuminated by fairy lights strung from the ceiling. It was magical and romantic.

"And Wyatt," Mason said.

Did she miss something?

"What about Wyatt?"

"Imagine my surprise when I met your date. I assumed you were coming alone."

Linda looked at the lapel of his jacket, not wanting to meet his eyes.

"I never said that I was."

"Right, but I was hoping I'd be your unofficial date."

"Mason," she began, in what was clearly a "It's not you, it's me" voice.

"Wait," he cut her off. "I have a few things to say."

There was something different in the tone of his voice. Linda raised her eyes, searching his. They were still swaying, but she couldn't hear the music.

"When you were in Seattle, I brought up the idea of staying. But I saw the look on your face when I did that. I realized that even though you were interested in visiting, you had no interest in staying. Even if I was there."

He paused. "I was caught up in the moment. Excited that you came to see me. But I let that excitement cloud what I knew: you love it here. This is home. Moving around seems normal to me, and I forget how unusual it is for most people."

"And I would never ask you to give up what makes you happy."

"I know you wouldn't. And I wouldn't ask you to. But here's the thing. You make me happy. Being with you makes me happy. And most importantly, making you happy makes me happy. I can work anywhere. What I can't do is be happy without you."

Linda bit her lip. His words were perfect and easy to say, but they weren't enough. She couldn't do a long-distance relationship. She didn't want a long-distance relationship. She had to tell him.

"I don't think I can do a long-distance relationship."

"Not asking you to. I'm coming home."

Her eyes widened. Had she heard him correctly?

"Home?" she whispered.

"Yes." He smiled. "I'm still looking for the right job here, but I've talked to my placement manager about getting closer in the meantime. We'll see what they come up with."

"Are you sure? What if you come back and you hate it?"

"How could I hate it? The only thing I would hate is if you didn't want to be with me. If you were interested in someone else, like Wyatt."

"No. How could I be? It's always been you."

He closed his eyes, resting his forehead on the top of her head, and pulled her closer. "I've known it was you since we were kids. It just took reconnecting for me to remember that. I pushed a lot of things out of my life so I wouldn't feel pain, but someone reminded me recently that life is not about avoiding the pain, it's about searching for the joy. And that's what I have when I'm with you."

She pulled back to search his eyes again. They reflected the love and devotion she felt for him. To share that with her best friend was everything.

"Now." Mason stopped dancing and pulled back from her. "Can we talk about what you've done with your hair? I can't believe she talked you into dyeing it."

Linda giggled. "I didn't."

Confusion crossed his face, and he shook his head. "But..."

Linda reached up and tugged lightly at the hairline. "It's a wig."

"No way! It looks real." He put his hand on his heart. "Thank goodness. I've been missing your pink hair all evening. When can you get rid of the wig?"

She shrugged. "Pictures are done..."

"Go. Go now!" he said, pointing towards the door.

"I'll be back."

Linda rushed to the bridal suite where they'd gotten ready. Her hands shook as she searched her hairline for the pins holding the wig in place, thankful she hadn't let the hairdresser use glue.

It took several minutes to get all the pins out and the wig off. She grabbed a can of dry shampoo, sprayed, and leaned over, flipping her hair upside down to add volume.

There was no time to curl it or make it fancy, but a few brush strokes made her presentable.

She reapplied her lipstick and turned towards the door. Doubt crept in. How long had Mason felt this way? Did he change his mind about traveling when she was in Seattle? Or was it driven by seeing her with Wyatt tonight? She took a moment to remind herself not to get caught up in the romance of the wedding. If Mason was serious, he'd take action. She could wait and see.

But maybe she needed to show Mason that she was serious about him, too. If he was willing to settle down, she could have a say about where. It didn't have to be here in central Illinois, though that's what she'd prefer. She wanted to be with Mason, and there was something she could do to prove it to him.

The timing was good. Now that Laurel's wedding was complete and Linda was making progress with her new line of business, it was time for a few more changes.

Chapter 28

Two weeks after Laurel's wedding, Mason finally found what he'd been scouring the internet for—a vintage, seventeen-foot Airstream camper. The previous owner had gutted it before deciding it was too big a job for him to tackle, saying he'd rather be fishing than restoring.

Being gutted seemed the ideal situation to Mason. Linda wouldn't be camping in it, and she didn't need a small kitchenette, a dining table, or a bed. She needed space for shelves and display racks and storage. It seemed perfect to him, but he'd called Nica to confer with her before making an offer. He bought it without having seen it in person. The camper was in Minnesota. After several more phone calls, he found a company to haul it to Bloomington.

He'd originally planned to meet his family over the Fourth of July weekend in Florida, but the camper took precedence. He wrapped his stint up in Seattle and flew back to central Illinois to do a walkthrough with Nica and to get her ideas before presenting it to Linda.

He didn't know how Linda was going to react. He assumed she'd protest profusely that he'd bought something so expensive for her, but he hoped that she'd come around and see that he wanted her to pursue her dream, and if he could help, he would.

Worst-case scenario, if she hated the idea, he would resell the camper.

He could not wait to surprise her. He hoped it would show her he was supporting her dream to launch her own line of stationery products and sell them at farmers' markets. She was the most important thing in the world to him, and he'd do whatever it took to make her happy. He hoped he'd be able to tell her he'd found a position in Bloomington next. Springfield was close, but not close enough.

Though Linda talked to and emailed Grady frequently, it was unusual to have face-to-face time with her boss, but she asked for a working-lunch meeting with him. She had a big announcement to make but she didn't tell him that piece of information before the meeting.

She arrived at the restaurant ten minutes early and asked to be seated right away. She wanted time to organize her things before Grady arrived.

There was the contract for the building on MacArthur Ave, which Linda had redlined for Grady to review. It had taken weeks, but when they found that Grady's offer had been accepted, even after Linda had turned it in late, Linda had cried with relief.

Then there was a list of suggestions submitted by his renters to review.

And finally, there was her resignation letter to give him.

She was nervous about giving him the letter, not just about his reaction to it, but about what was next for her. Going full-time on her side hustle was momentous. She was putting herself out there, and it felt like an enormous leap of faith. If she didn't "make it" with this venture, would she be able to work for Grady again?

Linda didn't hear Grady approach, and she shrieked when he slid into the booth across from her. "Yikes!"

"Hello." Grady's smirk told her he'd enjoyed surprising her. "Sorry to sneak up on you."

She pulled her hand away from her chest as her heart rate slowed. "Hi. I was getting organized here."

"You're always prepared. It's nice to see you in person. Nica and I had a great time at your sister's wedding."

"It was lovely, wasn't it?"

"It was. Kind of fun to watch the dynamics between your two dates," Grady teased.

"I just had one date!"

"Not from where I was sitting. I got to watch the two men assess each other over dinner. Lucky for you, they got along well."

"Yeah." Linda wasn't so sure. After her first dance with Mason, she'd pulled Wyatt aside and apologized for putting him in an awkward situation. Wyatt rolled with it and said that though he was bummed, he liked Mason and understood her decision. "So, did you ever interview Wyatt for a job at the bank?"

"I did. He starts on Monday."

"Wow. I hope it works out."

"Time will tell. Now, let's get to work. I only have an hour."

They'd gone over all the normal business as they ate. The server cleared their plates, and Grady dropped his credit card on the table, ready for the check.

"Um, Grady. I have one more thing."

She picked up the folder with her resignation letter and froze. This was even harder than she had imagined it would be.

He held her gaze, waiting patiently.

"I..." She felt the words choking her. "I've decided to focus on my side hustle, make it my career."

Grady nodded, not looking surprised, mad, or upset.

Linda continued. "I can't do that while I work full-time for you."

She felt a pit open in the bottom of her stomach and wished she'd done this before she ate.

Grady nodded again and held out his hand. She passed him the folder. Grady took it and set it on the seat next to him on top of the other paperwork she'd already given him.

He smiled and leaned forward. "I'm proud of you. You're going to do great things. How much longer do I have you for?"

"Three weeks?"

"All right. We'll make that work. Can you write up a transition plan with all the open items you're working on and recommendations on how best to hand them over? I'd appreciate it if you can close as many as you can."

She smiled. "I have that list started. I'll keep it updated until my last day, and we can go over it then." She sighed in relief. "That was easier than I expected. Thanks, Grady."

"I knew this day would come. Always plan for your contingencies." He smiled, his green eyes twinkling. He'd told her that so many times. "And let me know how I can help you get your business off the ground."

"I will. Should I create a job posting for an assistant?"

"Please do. Though I may have you hand a few things off to Wyatt in the meantime."

"Grady! No!"

He chuckled. "Got to get you back somehow for leaving me."

She smiled and shook her head. "Sounds about right."

Chapter 29

Preparing to leave her job with Grady occupied Linda's mind from sunup to sundown for two more weeks.

Mason had called her every day since Laurel's wedding, but recently the calls were hardly over five minutes.

He was moving to Springfield next week, and she was excited that he would be only an hour away. Her fears that his focus on her time zone could land him twenty hours away by car had not been realized.

He was flying home today and would stay with Erin for a few days. On Saturday, once Linda wrapped things up for Grady, the two of them would drive to Springfield to get Mason settled before his first shift the following Monday.

Linda offered to pick him up at the airport but he said he'd take a rideshare to Erin's and pick up Linda to have dinner.

She freshened up and put on makeup before Mason arrived. She'd cleared her work papers off the dining table and tidied up the apartment. Sorcha had gone to Chicago to visit the Art Institute and wouldn't be home until late.

When he knocked, Linda leaped off the couch and rushed to the door.

"Hi!" she said, throwing the door open.

Mason wore black slacks and a red short-sleeved polo shirt. Somehow, he looked relaxed and excited at the same time.

"Hello," he said, stepping through the door.

"You were vague about plans for this evening." She looked down at her pale blue sundress. "I wasn't sure if we would go out for dinner, or order in..."

"We're going to dinner. We have a stop to make on the way. Shouldn't take too long."

"Okay. Let me give you a quick tour of the apartment, then we can go."

She led him on the ninety-second tour of their humble two-bedroom apartment—not showing him Sorcha's room prevented the tour from going to ninety-five seconds.

Mason had rented a car but admitted he felt a little weird driving. "I'm looking for a car to purchase," he said, driving down Veteran's Parkway. "Springfield is not as large as most of the cities I've lived in, and besides, I'll just be an hour away. I don't want to rely on Amtrak to visit you, though that is an option."

"Really? I never think about taking a train."

"Not even going to Chicago?"

"Well, I've thought about it but never done it. Sorcha took the train to Chicago today, actually. I would have gone with her if you hadn't come in."

"We'll have to do that. Soon."

Linda loved his enthusiasm. "Sounds fun. I'd like that."

She was confused when he pulled into a flower shop parking lot a few minutes later. The shop didn't appear to be open. She was further surprised when he pulled up to the portico in front of the building.

"Mason, this place doesn't look open..."

It was nice that he'd thought of flowers, but shouldn't he have brought them to her door?

"The surprise is here. Come on."

He bounced out of the car and rushed around to her side. Taking her hand, he led her around the building.

"Are we trespassing?" she asked, glancing around. There were no other cars around, just a large metal camper that looked like it had been in the woods recently.

Mason led her towards the camper. Turning to her, he said, "Linda, this may seem a little crazy but hear me out. I got this idea when I talked to Nica at the wedding. You said you want to attend farmers' markets to sell your new products."

"Yeah…." Linda's eyes darted from Mason to the camper behind him.

"Well, here's your booth for those markets. It needs work, obviously, but Nica has seen it, and she's drawing up some ideas now to go over with you."

"Mason, I can't—" There were so many "I can'ts": "I can't accept this", "I can't haul this", "I can't park this in my apartment's parking lot", "I can't…." But the "I coulds" slowly filtered in.

"Yes, you can. If you hate this idea, that's fine. I'll resell it. But think about it. You'll be able to go to lots of markets on the weekends. It will be functional and adorable. Whatever you want. Nica thinks you could arrange with the owner of the flower shop to park here and cross-promote your businesses. Tilly, the owner, was fine with it being parked here for a few days to start with. Nica said you probably know of some other places that Grady owns if it doesn't work here, since you know all your boss's locations."

"Mason, about that."

She'd planned to tell him at dinner that she was quitting her job with Grady and going full-time on her new venture. But now that it had come up…

"I've turned in my resignation with Grady. Mainly to work on my business full-time, but partially to have the flexibility to move to wherever you settle." She snickered. "When you settle."

"No way! I can't believe you'd do that." He looked down at his feet for a second. "You didn't have to do that, Lindy. I'm moving back here as soon as I can. Springfield is just a stepping-stone. I want to be with you. And I know you love it here. I just want to be where you are. They say home is where the heart is. Well, my heart is with you. Your heart is my home."

"Mason." Her voice shook. This was too much to take in. Mason was coming home! She took a deep breath and stepped into his arms. "You're moving back here? For good?"

She felt his quiet chuckle from his chest through hers. "For good. It's time. I want to be with you. And I want to be close to my family. None of us are getting younger, and I have some lost time to make up for."

"No time like the present."

"Exactly."

Linda's eyes shifted from him to the camper. "So, Nica thinks we can make this into a vendor booth, huh?"

"Ready to see it?"

"Can't wait."

EPILOGUE

Four months later…

Most of their immediate family members were in Seaside Bay for Thanksgiving. Erin would fly down Friday morning, since she had to work the holiday. Laurel and Patrick were renting Ms. Esquivel's condo, while she was visiting family in New Mexico. Uncle Paul and Aunt Sandy were staying in their condo and hosting the twins' parents for the holiday, which meant Linda was sleeping on the couch. At least she wasn't having a slumber party with her twin and her twin's new husband in the living room.

Since Erin was arriving later than everyone else, they planned their big homemade meal for Saturday. On Thanksgiving Day, the Brees and Hauser families ordered Chinese takeout.

Linda stuffed herself with fried rice and egg rolls. After dinner, when Mason suggested a walk on the beach, Linda jumped at the chance to get outside for fresh air and spend some alone time with Mason.

"Look!" Mason pointed ahead of them to where a large group gathered on the beach. "It looks like a party."

As they neared, the sound of a young girl singing and playing guitar wafted towards them. "She's pretty good," Linda noted.

"Yeah."

"Want to hang out here and listen?"

"No, let's keep walking."

They continued past the small crowd gathered around a bonfire. As they approached, the guitar passed to a man who played a Neil Young song.

"Doesn't feel like Thanksgiving," Linda said. This was the first time in over ten years that the family had traveled to Florida for the holiday. Her mom preferred to be home and host in her own kitchen. But now that Laurel was married, they all agreed that it was time for some new traditions.

"I agree! No turkey, no holiday. Just like Erin, throwing a wrench into our plans."

"Watch it, Mister. Next year, it might be you working on the holiday."

Mason had recently accepted a permanent position at a hospital in Bloomington. He wouldn't start until the first of the year, as he needed to wrap up his last rotational stint in Springfield and move back home. Linda had reached out to Grady's new assistant to locate a rental for Mason. They'd been ecstatic to find one just three blocks from Linda's apartment.

"That's true. Are you going to regret dating someone who works crazy hospital hours, on-call shifts, and holidays?" Mason's eyes were serious, but his tone was light.

"If it's you, no. Never. We just need to communicate and have a shared calendar."

"A digital calendar, right? Not a printable," he teased.

"Fine," she quipped back. "Digital it is. Whatever, as long as you're happy."

Mason chuckled and walked a few more steps. "Can't believe we're finally going to be living in the same city again. I'm excited about the future."

As waves lapped her feet, Linda felt a wave of contentment wash over her. She was excited about the holidays and the year ahead. She'd be able to see Mason most days of the week. Her stationery business was taking off, and she was contemplating opening her own retail store.

"I am, too." She paused. "I can't wait for you to move closer. It feels sort of surreal right now. The past few months since you've been in Springfield have been wonderful. Seeing you at least once a week, sometimes twice, was great. But seeing you nightly will be even better. I've been searching for new recipes. I promise I'm going to learn how to cook. You will have the bigger kitchen, and you won't have a roommate, so I was thinking we could make dinner at your place most nights. That would be good for me, too, because I'm working from home, and I get a little stir-crazy when I feel like I'm stuck at home all the time."

I'm rambling. I probably didn't need that second diet cola at dinner; the caffeine surge is racing through me.

Mason stopped and turned towards her. "I like the sound of that. But you know what would be even better?"

"What?" *I said I would learn to cook. What could be better than that?*

"When we live together, and you don't have to come over every night to make dinner."

"Sure, but I would still need an office to go to, so I'm not home all the time. Tilly's fiancé has a coworking office space. I could probably rent out a space there. She was telling me about it last weekend. A lot of professionals and creatives use it."

While she was chatting about office space, Mason knelt in the sand. "Hey, you're going to get sand on your jeans," she said, before it occurred to her that Mason wasn't simply taking a rest.

"Lindy," Mason said, beaming. "Before we move in together, I was hoping you'd traipse down an aisle with me. You're my best friend, and you have been for a long time. Even when we were apart, I always thought of you as my best friend. I pretended that I'd be seeing you soon. It was easier to pretend than to face the fact that I'd screwed up and let you go."

He reached into his pocket and pulled out a ring box. "I hope, in all our future days together I can show you how much you mean to me. I will strive to make you feel honored, cherished, and loved. Because I love you. I want to see you every day, not most days. And not just for dinner. Breakfast and lunch, too, when we can."

He took a deep breath. "Will you marry me?"

Before she could answer, he continued, "Before I open this ring box, know that it is a placeholder. I've looked at rings, and I think I know what you'd like, but I wasn't one hundred percent certain, so I want to go shopping with you, and let you pick the ring you love best. What do you say?"

Linda smiled. "To the proposal or ring shopping?"

"Are there different answers?"

She laughed. "No. Same answer to both. A resounding yes!"

He stood, wrapping her in his arms.

She squeezed him as she rested her head on his chest. *This is incredible. How did I get so lucky? Not just reuniting with Mason but giving him my heart again. I think I stood on this very spot six months ago and told myself not to fall in love with him again. But now look at us. We're going to get married! Yippee!*

Someone yelled, "Congratulations! I guess she said yes!"

Mason pulled back a few inches and searched for the passerby. "She did! Lucky me!"

His lips brushed hers, and she answered by rising on her toes to deepen the kiss. Kissing him here reminded her of their very first kiss at fifteen—on this beach, close to the same spot.

She pulled back. "Mason, do you remember our first kiss?"

He smiled. "Of course. It was right here. That's why I chose this spot to propose. See?" He turned and pointed to the large purple manatee statue that stood next to the door of a charming boutique hotel.

"You're right! We were racing to see who could reach this spot first. I won."

"No, I won." His eyes widened. "I got a kiss that night."

"OK. It was a tie. We both won."

"Still winning. Let's go back. I can't wait to tell everyone and get out the champagne I bought."

He took her hand and started walking.

"Did your family know you were proposing?" she asked.

"No." He chuckled. "I couldn't bear the humiliation if you said no. But I don't think they'll be surprised."

"Well, let's go tell them. Then I have a phone call to make."

Everyone gathered in the Hauser's condo to toast the engagement. Mason called Erin and put her on a video call to share the news.

After the excitement settled down, Linda excused herself to make a phone call.

She stepped out onto the balcony and pulled the door shut behind her. The sun had set, and the sky seemed to celebrate her news with an abundance of glittering stars. It reminded her of a story or a movie where the stars spoke to each other, but she could not remember the reference.

Sorcha answered her call on the second ring, and Linda could hear music and people talking in the background.

"Sorcha, I have news! Can you talk for a minute?"

"Hold on. Hold on." There was a ruffling noise and then the background noise dimmed. "Okay, I popped into the pantry. What's going on? Happy Turkey Day, by the way."

"Right. Gobble, gobble." She took a deep breath. "Mason proposed!"

"What?" Sorcha practically screamed into the phone. "Oh my gosh, I'm so, so, so happy for you! Called it. I woke up this morning and said something fantastic was going to happen today. I was hoping it might happen to me..." She paused for dramatic effect. "But you getting engaged is just as good. Congratulations!"

Linda laughed. "There are hours left in the day. Don't give up hope just yet."

"Right. Hey, send me a picture of the ring. Now!"

"About that..." Linda paused and took a picture of the plastic ring with the glittery pink seashell on it. She sent the picture and waited for Sorcha to open it.

"Um, that's the ring?"

"Yes," Linda giggled. "He wants me to pick out my engagement ring. He picked this up in a tourist shop yesterday. I don't know. I think it's adorable."

"Cute, yes. Engagement, no. Ooh, I'll help you shop. We're going to Tiffany's!"

"I'm in no hurry to replace this ring. I like it."

A knock on the patio door caused Linda to turn around. Mason shrugged his shoulders and pretended to pout.

"Hey," Linda continued. "I should get back to the impromptu engagement party inside. But I couldn't wait to share the news with you. I was thinking we should plan a girls' weekend at the beach soon to do some wedding planning."

"How soon are you thinking? The holidays are coming up, and I'm busy through January..."

"Maybe spring break."

"That would work if you're not in a big hurry."

"It'll be fine. Maybe love will find *you* on our next trip to Seaside Bay. It worked for me."

Sorcha clicked her tongue. "Not so fast. I've given up on love. I'm going to run off and join the circus."

"Never give up on love! I suspect that the good feeling you had this morning is going to turn into love soon."

"We'll see. Get back to your party, Lulu. I'll see you soon."

Linda hung up and inhaled the refreshing cool air coming from the Gulf.

I can't believe I'm engaged! Telling Sorcha made it even more real. There's so much to do. I need to make a list. Loving the idea of a girls' getaway in the spring. Though I may have all the wedding details planned out by then. Which would be good, because I'm on a mission to find a man for Sorcha. Someone who will appreciate all the things that make her great!

Linda made the decision to turn her side hustle into her main hustle. See her get ready for the store's grand opening in the bonus epilogue. In addition to seeing her store on wheels and catching up with Linda and Mason months after the end of "Poolside Promises", you also receive several of Linda's printables. Click here to get the bonus epilogue https://dl.bookfunnel.com/VP9849 N5GF. You can also get these fun printable planners on my website, https://www.kasey-kennedy.com, go to the "Fun Stuff" tab.

Linda is excited to plan a girls' weekend trip with Sorcha and Laurel to plan her wedding to Mason. When the ladies return to Seaside Bay, Sorcha declares she's done with love, but is love done with her? You'll find out in *Beachside Bliss* which will launch in early 2025. Pre-order it now so you don't forget! https://www.amazon.com/dp/B0DC5XZHPG

At Laurel's wedding, Mason chatted with Nica about a store on wheels for Linda. Nica mentioned her former boss, Anna Lee, and the floral shop, In Bloom, where Mason initially parks the trailer for Linda.

Anna Lee is a spitfire and loves nurturing the young ladies who work for her. You can get a free introductory novella to the In Bloom series, here https://dl.bookfun nel.com/2t55c02zjm where you meet Anna Lee, Paige, Nica, Lauren, and Tilly. The In Bloom series is full of stories about finding yourself in this world, and finding someone you can fall madly in love with!

You can jump into the In Bloom series by checking out book 1, *Peonies for Paige*, on Amazon https://www.amaz on.com/dp/B0B8GD3H1K. She's dreaming of the big city. He just wants to settle down. They've planted love, but can they tend it long enough to reap forever?

ACKNOWLEDGEMENTS

First, I want to thank my husband, Tim, for supporting my writing dream. Thank you for being my sounding board, my inspiration, and my champion. I don't know what I would do without you. I love you!

A huge shout out to Patty B, Chris B, Kristina, and Jill H for beta reading—thank you for your comments and attention to detail!

Thank you to Lindsey at Word Nerd Author Services for supporting this release and pulling together the team of amazing and engaged ARC Readers!

To the team of ARC Readers – thank you for reading and sharing this story. It was wonderful getting to "meet" you all and seeing your beautiful, creative posts!

Thank you to the writing friends who encourage me and hold my feet to the fire: Lynn, Rebecca, Emily, Trish, Stephanie, Bryn, and so many others. I appreciate you and am always here to cheer you on!

Family is everything, and I want to thank my siblings, siblings-in-law, aunts, uncles, cousins, nieces, and nephews for all the encouragement. I love you infinitely.

Thank you to the professionals who supported this project—Marisa F for Development Editing, Rebecca H for copy editing, Stacy U for proofreading, and Deborah Bradseth for the gorgeous book cover!

And a heartfelt thank you to you, dear reader, for taking a chance on this story.

ABOUT THE AUTHOR

Kasey Kennedy is an Illinois gal through and through. She grew up in Central Illinois, finished college at Southern Illinois University Carbondale, and, soon afterward, moved to Chicago. She's been in Chicago or the surrounding suburbs ever since.

Kasey is happily married to her husband Tim and loves spending time with him—especially when that involves live music! If not attending a live show, they are usually enjoying evenings on the deck, listening to music, visiting their large families, watching movies, or planning their next trip.

When not dreaming up new characters and new stories, Kasey is reading or planning what to read next. Occasionally, she pulls out the guitar that she has been trying to learn for 30+ years and strums enough to annoy her cat, Pepper.

Keep in touch on social media:
https://www.facebook.com/kaseykennedy8/
https://www.instagram.com/kaseykennedy8
Visit my website to sign up for my newsletter.
website https://www.kasey-kennedy.com

www.ingramcontent.com/pod-product-compliance
Lightning Source LLC
Chambersburg PA
CBHW031558310726
48974CB00003B/721